STEPBROTHE

CW01497489

By Colleen Masters

Also From Colleen Masters:

Stepbrother Billionaire by Colleen Masters

Faster Harder (Take Me... #1) by Colleen Masters

Faster Deeper (Take Me... #2) by Colleen Masters

Faster Longer (Take Me... #3) by Colleen Masters

Faster Hotter (Take Me...#4) by Colleen Masters

Faster Dirtier (Take Me...#5) (A Team Ferrelli Novel) by Colleen Masters

* * *

DEDICATION

To all my beautiful readers.

Join thousands of our readers on the mailing list to receive FREE copies of our new books!

CLICK HERE TO JOIN NOW

We will never spam you – Feel free to unsubscribe anytime!

Connect with Colleen Masters and other Hearts Collective authors online at: http://www.Hearts-Collective.com, Facebook, Twitter. To keep in touch and for information on new releases!

STEPBROTHER UNTOUCHABLE

* * *

by Colleen Masters

CONTENTS

CHAPTER ONE

* * *

I bounce from foot to foot as I try my mom's cell phone one more time. I'm practically bursting at the seams wanting to tell her my good news, and she's not answering. I hang up the call as it goes to her voicemail again. She's been a little more unreachable ever since she started dating this new mystery man. She'll have to break down and tell me about him soon—we've never been able to keep secrets from one another for long.

I give up and hold down the number 2 button on my old flip-phone to auto-dial my best friend Allison. Thankfully, she picks up.

"I got it! I got a Lawn Room!" I shriek as soon as she answers, my excitement overflowing into a wild jig around my tiny dorm room. Allison screams on the other end in response—she knows what a huge deal this is for me.

There are only fifty-four Lawn Rooms at the University of Virginia, where I'm just finishing my junior year. They were a central part of Thomas Jefferson's design for the school, and spread out under white columns from his famous Rotunda. They might be small and drafty, but living in one is a high honor. There's a rigorous application process, and they are given to only the most academically-deserving rising seniors. I worked my nerdy butt off in preparation for this moment, and I can barely believe it's actually happening.

"Wait, wait, I'm putting you on speaker. Miriam's here, too," Allison says when she finally takes a breath. Miriam is the third member of our little group that I met freshman year, and has both supported me and sheltered me through the first three years of college.

"Brynn, I'm so proud of you! I mean, think of how many hundreds and hundreds of hours you worked for this moment!" she gushes.

I laugh. "Don't remind me!" I wince, thinking of how much of college life I've missed while huddled in the back stacks of the library. Not that Miriam and Allison are academic slouches either, far from it, all three of us could probably draw you a map of the library from memory.

"And if it gets too cold in the winter, you can always come crash with us," Allison adds. She and Miriam have been roommates since sophomore year, and will be again next year. They've always invited me to apply for housing with them, but after freshman year, I decided I was too much of an introvert for roommates.

"The fireplace is probably the best and worst part of the whole thing," I laugh. The Lawn rooms have almost no trappings of the modern world, so in the winter all you have to keep yourself warm is your own personal fireplace. It sounds romantic now, but come next January, I imagine I might feel differently.

"Are you working tonight? Or can we celebrate?" Miriam asks. I work in the cafeteria as part of my work-study program to offset the cost of my tuition.

"Maybe we could go to dinner together, then see a movie?"

"Well, I'm not working," I admit, guilt already bubbling up from my stomach, "but I was thinking I might go out with these girls from my Poli-Sci class."

There's a short silence before Allison speaks. "Oh, cool…Sounds fun. What are you guys going to do?"

"Um, they invited me to this party at the crew house," I say, beginning to tug on the ends of my dark blonde hair—a nervous habit that only really gets out of control during finals.

"The crew house!?" Allison exclaims, and I can't help but roll my eyes at her theatrics. "Brynn, you know as well as we do that those parties get insane! I heard that last semester NINE of their varsity members got alcohol poisoning in one night!"

"Well, there are only eight on a team, so I think that might be an exaggeration," I murmur. "Though I suppose maybe an alternate—"

"Brynn, the point is, those parties are notoriously crazy," Miriam cuts in.

"I just want to see for myself," I say, trying to keep the frustration out of my voice. "I'll call you guys tomorrow morning."

"OK…" Allison says warily.

"Bye!" I say quickly, before Miriam can renew her argument, and hang up.

As wonderful as my two best friends are, I do get tired of how uptight they can be sometimes. Not that I don't understand where it comes from. The three of us weren't exactly popular during high school, and when we found each other during our freshman year orientation, it was such an amazing relief to be with like-minded girls. We were all serious students, driven, with a penchant for fantasy books that might star Viggo Mortensen in the movie adaption.

But now, I'm beginning to chafe at the boundaries of our friendship. Particularly when it comes to going out to parties, and boys. On my early morning trips to the library, I see girls doing the walk of shame across campus, their makeup smeared across their faces, hair rumpled, and first I feel pity, and then intense jealousy. That post-sex glazed over look…if I'm honest with myself, I want that too.

And I promised myself that if I got my Lawn Room, I'd go to a party. A real college party. The kind Miriam and Allison roll their eyes at as they wonder how many brain cells its attendees are killing by the second. This crew party is the perfect opportunity. I'm trying not to get my hopes up, but it remains a possibility that I might actually get to talk to Nate Thornhill tonight.

Just the thought of his name is enough to send tingles down my spine, though I know the real-life man could probably never live up to the fantasy I've built up in my mind. I still remember the first time I saw him, walking across campus the second weekend of fall semester of freshman year. I would've bet my life then that he was a senior. Compared to the boys I had just left behind in high school, he was already a full-grown man. He wore a navy blue polo like it was a second skin as he strode across the grass, Jefferson's Palladian architecture spread out behind him like it was built as a set for a movie he was starring in. He wore his wavy brown hair on the long side, and pushed back to keep it out of his dark blue eyes. His nose was perfectly straight and ended over a pair of soft, full lips and a chin with an actual dimple in it. If it were possible for Ryan Gosling and a Kennedy to have a baby, the result would be Nate Thornhill.

I later learned that he was a double major like me, and since one of mine is Political Science and one of his is History, we overlapped in a few of our core courses. I expected him to sit in the back with the rest of the jocks but he was always in the front row, quick to raise his hand with intelligent answers. I always hide right in the center of the halls; my shyness overwhelms me in those big lecture classes. I've never got up the courage to actually talk to him, and besides, he always has a different girl on his arm. With his looks, money, and being a star of both the lacrosse and crew teams, he draws women in like a magnet.

But tonight? Tonight I have promised myself that if he's at the party, I am going to introduce myself.

I shoot off a quick text to Cara, my new friend from class, to confirm that I'll join her tonight, and then turn to my closet. I really only have one option to wear tonight: a simple, slinky black camisole with a lace inlay that I bought at the mall in spite of Miriam and Allison's naysaying. I didn't know what I was buying it for then, but it's the kind of shirt I've seen other girls wearing to parties. I slip on jeans and a pair of heels that are probably a little low to be cool, but they'll have to do. It's not like I have extra money to be adding to my wardrobe.

I take out the drug store makeup that I bought and sit at my desk. I never usually wear anything but Chapstick, but I watched some YouTube tutorials and feel confident I can mimic some of the techniques. With a compact mirror, I carefully put on a little concealer, blush, brown eye shadow, and black mascara. I bought an eyeliner, but I don't use it. I think it's a little beyond my skills. With a swipe of some sparkly lip gloss, I'm done.

I close the closet door and study myself in the full-length mirror. With a start, I recognize myself in the reflection. I turn my face side to side, searching for all its imperfections. With a little makeup on, my resemblance to my mom is more pronounced. Everyone always says she is beautiful, so maybe it's possible that I might be pretty, too. The shirt is more low-cut than I remembered, and I touch my breasts self-consciously. I get my large C-cups from my mom also, but I've always kept them covered up. I see how men get distracted by them, like they're some tractor beam pulling them in.

One more quick glance to check my mascara application, and I nod at myself, satisfied. It's been a long time coming, but I think I'm finally ready to party.

CHAPTER TWO

∗ ∗ ∗

The spring night air is warm on my face as I walk across campus to meet Cara and her friends. I pass other students heading out for the night and feel happy to count myself among them. I go over my rules for myself as I near the crew house, which is just across the street from campus. No more than three drinks. No talking about classes. No weirdness around Nate Thornhill.

"Brynn!" Cara yells from the opposite sidewalk. I wave as I head over. "I can't believe you got a Lawn Room! That's amazing!" I lean over to give her a hug. She's an effortlessly cool, petite brunette—the kind of girl that everyone considers to be their friend.

"Thanks!"

"Holy shit! You got a Lawn Room? Are you, like, a genius or something?" her friend Rachel asks, her jaw dropping.

"I wish! Then all those papers would have taken me way less time to write," I reply with a laugh.

"Cara says you've never been to a crew party?" Marie, the knockout of the group, asks.

"Nope…just never made my way over here I guess," I reply, downplaying the situation.

"Well, they have the best parties," she assures me. "And the hottest guys."

"Lacrosse guys are hotter," Rachel argues.

"Of course, if you can always do both…" Marie murmurs, and they burst into laughter.

"Hey, you look great, by the way," Cara says to me as we walk up the front steps of the house. "Love that top."

"Thanks," I say, trying not to glow. A couple guys chilling on the front porch greet the other girls by name, and I blush as I feel their eyes glance over me. I tug my hair self-consciously as one of them grins at me. Two girls hurry past us in the opposite direction. One leans over the railing as her friend barely manages to pull her hair back before she retches into the bushes.

Lovely.

Sweat and the scent of beer greets us as we walk inside. The lights are dim, barely illuminating the mass of people crowded into the main room, and I feel my heels sticking to the sticky floor.

"Cara, the love of my life!" a tall, brawny guy says, sweeping her up into a hug. I recognize him from the crew team. Not that I've studied their roster photos or anything…

"Oh, ha, ha," Cara says, rolling her eyes, though something about the gleam in her eyes tells me she likes the guy.

"Can I get you ladies a beer?" he asks, nodding to the keg behind him.

"Yes, please," Cara says. "Hey, Foster, this is my good friend Brynn. This is her first Crew party so treat her nice."

"I'm always nice!" Foster says indignantly, then bows in front of me and offers his hand. "M'lady," he says, as I place my hand in his and raises it to his lips. Marie and Rachel giggle and then head over to another group as Foster hands them their beers. Cara and I follow Foster over to an old, mysteriously stained, couch in the corner. We weave around other scantily clad co-eds, and for the first time in my life, I feel like one of the cool kids.

I perch nervously on the far left cushion as Cara sits next to me, with Foster on her other side. I slowly sip my beer as he whispers in her ear. I've had beer before, even gotten tipsy a few times with Allison and Miriam when we first turned twenty-one and tried out some wine bars. I just want to make sure I don't overdo it tonight and end up like that girl we passed on the way inside.

"Where's Nate tonight?" My head whips around as I hear Cara ask Foster the question. My heart stops for a second. I have to admit I'll feel crushed if he's not even here.

"He's somewhere around, probably getting crushed under a pile of chicks," Foster rolls his eyes, and Cara laughs. I down half my beer. I can't believe how jealous it makes me feel, I've never even met the guy.

Cara and Foster keep chatting, and though Cara makes an effort to include me, I'm feeling too nervous to contribute much to the conversation. By the time I finish my beer, I really have to pee.

"Be right back," I murmur to Cara, and go looking for the bathroom. I weave through the sweaty throng to a hallway along the stairs. I see a line of five girls outside of what I assume is the bathroom, and with a sigh, I step behind the last one. The door opens and a guy darts in front of the front girl.

"Hey!" she protests.

"Sorry! Emergency!" he cries, and shuts the door behind him. I lean back a little and glance up the stairs. There are several people hanging out on the landing, but it's definitely quieter up there, and I'm sure there's more than one bathroom in this place. Holding my legs close together, I turn around and hurry up the stairs.

I bypass the first couple rooms with open doors and come to a couple closed ones. I can see a room at the end of the hall that looks like a lounge, with a pool table in the middle of the room. One of these two rooms must be the bathroom. I lean toward the nearest one and press my ear against it. I can't hear anything. I knock softly and wait for a reply, and when I don't hear one, I slowly turn the knob and open the door. I gasp as it's pulled open and out of my grasp.

My eyes fly up and immediately I realize that Nate is standing before me.

"I…I…" I stammer. His pupils dilate as he stares at me in amusement. I let my gaze fall down his body. He's naked but for a pair of pale blue boxers. Good lord, his body is ridiculous. The line down between his six-pack looks like it was etched in stone. It's suddenly very difficult to breathe.

"See anything you like?" he asks drily. I snap my gaze back up. A brown curl of hair hangs just over one of his eyes. I clear my throat as I try to think of something to say. I feel his eyes travelling over my body, my skin burning under his gaze as desire begins to pool in my stomach.

"Oh, no, I was—"

"You wanna join us?" he says, pulling the door open a little more. I glance over his shoulder and see a naked girl in bed covered in rumpled sheets.

"Nate!" the girl says with a giggle, and pulls a sheet up over her breasts.

"Come on. If I weren't already naked, I'd say you were undressing me with your eyes," he says smugly to me. I feel my cheeks turn scarlet.

"No, sorry," I murmur, averting my eyes and rushing down the hall to the stairs as I hear the girl dissolve into laughter behind me. I run straight out of the front door and down the front steps before stopping on the sidewalk to process what's just happened.

Ugh, I'm such an idiot. I raise my hand to my mouth and wipe the back of my palm across my lips, smearing off my lip gloss. I don't belong at parties like this, and I certainly don't belong with Nate Thornhill. I've never been so embarrassed in my life…and how arrogant, asking me to join him and that girl as though I actually would?

Hot tears build up behind my eyes and threaten to spill over. I had such high hopes for tonight, such high hopes for *him*. And he ended up being so gross.

I pull my phone out of my wristlet and shoot off a quick text to Cara: *Hey, just got a terrible headache. Headed back to my dorm. See you later!*

I head back across campus and to the safety of my dorm room. My phone buzzes and I pull it back out to see her response: *Feel better!*

I envy Cara. Everything seems to come so easy to her. She can fit in anywhere, make friends with anyone. I guess I'm just not that kind of person, much as I'd like to be.

CHAPTER THREE

* * *

The words are a blur on the page in front of me. I rub my eyes. I didn't sleep well last night, and now I can't concentrate on my notes. We have a few days off at the beginning of the week to study, and then final exams. I can't let myself slip just because I got a Lawn Room, but the events of last night are distracting me and studying right now is nearly impossible.

My phone rings on the desk next to me.

"Hey, Mom!" I say as I pick up.

"Hey, honey! I just saw you called me a bunch yesterday! I'm sorry. I was out with Pierce." Her melodic voice sounds a little breathless, as it always does when she talks about this new boyfriend.

"Well, I have some good news."

"Me, too!" she replies.

"Oh! Um, do you want to go first?"

"Actually, I'm going to be in town tonight. Pierce and I were hoping to have dinner with you."

"You're in town?! That's great news."

She laughs. "No, that's not the news! Do you want to wait to tell me your news until then?"

"Um, sure. Why not? Everything's OK, though, right?"

"Everything's great! We have a reservation for 7 o'clock at Decanter. Should we pick you up?"

"No, that's OK. It's just a short walk from campus."

"Wonderful! Oh, I'm so excited to see you!" she says.

"Me too!"

I shut my phone feeling dumbfounded. Now I'm really not going to be able to study. My mom's never surprised me like this before. I frown. Could she and Pierce be engaged, and she wants to tell me in person? I guess I'd be happy for her, but I've never met this guy before. What if he's just one more jerk in the long line of lowlifes that she seems to attract?

My mom is so gorgeous and always loved the attention her looks brought her, but her vanity has always worried me. Men are so willing to do everything for her, but they never seem to be the right kind of men. Regardless of their character, she's always had a constant stream of admirers, and has never had to do anything for herself. She doesn't know who she is or how to be alone.

When I came along, my dad showed his true colors and abandoned us, and she had no skills to fall back on as a twenty-two year-old single mother. I always promised myself that I wouldn't let myself depend on a man like her. I had to make sure I could make my own way in the world, which is probably why I've had my nose in a book my whole life.

After several more hours of fruitless study, I decide to get ready a little early so that I can take a walk around campus before I meet my mom and her new boyfriend. I put on a cotton summer dress and grab a cardigan in case the restaurant is chilly.

I start to feel a little calmer when I reach the lawn and see the Rotunda's white dome in front of me. The architecture always inspires me, and next year I'll actually be living here. I stand in front of the women's side of the Lawn—genders are separated—and wonder which room will be mine.

My mind drifts back unbidden to last night. I so hoped to be able to expand my horizons a little. As wonderful as I know getting a Lawn room is, it's not everything.

The way Nate's body looked in the low light from the hall…the small tuft of hair that showed just above his boxers…the way he looked at me. I realize I'm tugging at my braid absent-mindedly, and shake my head at myself—I need to get it together. It's time to meet my mom and her new boyfriend, and hear their big news.

I glance around as I enter Decanter. Its architecture is modern and elegant, a mix of cream fabrics and dark wood. I've never been here before—way out of my price range. I'm about to approach the hostess when I recognize my mom in a prime booth in the corner. I walk toward her between a row of tables, hearing the hushed tones of conversation and the clinking of wine glasses around me.

Her eyes light up and she stands as she sees me approaching. She looks even more gorgeous than usual. Her blonde hair, a little lighter than mine, hangs in a long bob almost to her shoulders, and her perfect teeth show brightly behind her deep red lipstick.

"Brynn! I've missed you, honey," she says, enveloping me in a hug. "You look gorgeous. Isn't this dress a little big for you, though?" she asks, pulling at the extra fabric.

"You know I like this kind of fit," I reply, allowing only the slightest bit of impatience to enter my voice. This is a recurring conversation with us. She always wants me to dress a little more feminine, a little more "form-flattering" as she puts it.

"Well, I'm so excited for you to meet Pierce. He's just in the restroom—oh! Here he is." I follow her gaze to an elegantly dressed man with salt-and-pepper hair and blue eyes who's approaching us with a warm smile.

"Holly, I'd think this was your sister if I didn't know any better," he says, and my mom giggles. "Brynn, I'm Pierce. Your mom has told me such wonderful things about you," he says as we shake hands.

"Likewise," I reply politely, though the truth is that she's told me almost nothing.

"Well, let's sit. I ordered us some champagne for the table. It should be arriving soon." We all obediently sit, me on one side of the cushy leather booth, and my mom and Pierce on the other. "So, Brynn, you're in your junior year?"

"Yes, that's—" I break off as my mom reaches for her water glass and I spot a ring on her left hand. Not an engagement ring, either. A wedding ring. "What's that?" I ask sharply.

"Oh," my mom flutters.

"Well, we were going to wait until my son arrived, but—"

"We're married!" my mom announces suddenly.

My jaw drops open. "*Married?*" I squeak. "I mean, I thought *maybe* you'd be engaged but *married?*"

"You're upset?" my mom asks worriedly.

"No, not upset…" I struggle to put my emotions into the right words. I always feel the need to protect my mom from what I'm really feeling. She's always been more fragile than me. "Just surprised, that's all. I mean, how long have you known each other?"

"Well, we met six months ago," my mom says. "And then Pierce took me on a surprise trip to the Turks and Caicos last week, and everything was just so perfect…" She trails off, looking to him for support.

"It really was, Brynn. And it felt so right. We wished you guys could have been there, but we just felt that we had to seize the moment. It was in this little gazebo on the cliff, with spectacular views of the water, and the captain of a boat that was docked at the resort officiated…"

"It was engagement, honeymoon, and wedding in one! We just wished you and Nate could have been there. That would have made it even more perfect."

I struggle to catch up with all the information they're throwing at me. "Sorry, who's Nate?"

"Oh, Nate's my son. He goes to school here, too. I tried to get a hold of him so we could tell you together, but—wait! There he is!" Pierce slides out of the booth to wave to his son.

Nate. Not Nate…

"What's Pierce's last name?" I whisper urgently to my mom.

"Thornhill," she whispers back distractedly, sliding over to stand next to Pierce.

Oh my god. Nate Thornhill is here. Nate Thornhill is currently walking up behind me. *Nate Thornhill is my new…stepbrother*, I realize in horror. Beads of sweat form at my hairline and I've suddenly lost my appetite.

CHAPTER FOUR

* * *

As Nate walks into my periphery, I watch in slow motion as he hugs his dad and shakes hands with my mom. I cannot believe this is happening. Surely I'm in the middle of some strange nightmare and will wake up soon. I hoped I'd never have to see him again after last night.

"Brynn, honey, this is Nate, Pierce's son," my mom says, cutting through the fog of emotion in my brain.

"H-Hi. Nate. Brynn. I'm Brynn," I stammer as he glances over at me.

"Brynn, pleasure to meet you," he replies formally. Wait, does he not even remember meeting me last night?

"Well, scooch over Brynn, so Nate can sit," Mom says, waving me over with her hands.

"Right, sorry," I say, sliding over so that he can sit next to me. I stare straight ahead as he sits. I can feel my body betraying me already. The heat from his leg under the table is giving me heart palpitations.

"Thought you weren't going to be able to make it," Pierce says a little tensely to his son.

"Sorry, I was in the library studying. I had my phone off."

"Well, you missed the big announcement. We were just telling Brynn that Holly and I have gotten married."

I glance at Nate out of the corner of my eye. I see his eyes widen in surprise.

"Married? I thought you said you'd never get married again."

"Well, things change. When I met Holly, I just knew. You'll see when you get to know her. She's a special woman."

I watch my mom glow like a 1000 watt bulb and can't help but smile. It's been a while since I've seen her so happy.

"Yeah, I'm…I'm just…" I watch him struggle for words just like I did. "Surprised. But happy. I'm looking forward to getting to know you better, Holly."

Wow, that was…kind. Not what the guy I met last night would say.

"Oh, me too, Nate," my mom replies, looking overjoyed. "And I'm so excited for you and Brynn to get to know each other!"

"Two only children…" Pierce says meaningfully. "You'll have to learn to share."

My mom laughs and I join in weakly.

"You always wanted a sibling, Brynn! And now you have one! Well, a step-sibling, but still."

A step-sibling that I've had literally dozens of dirty dreams about. Perfect.

"So, you two have never met, then?" my mom asks, glancing between us. "Pierce and I were so excited when we realized both our kids were juniors here."

"UVA is my alma mater," Pierce adds proudly.

"No, we've never met," I break in quickly. I see Nate eye me for a second before he nods.

"Nope, never met, unfortunately," he says.

"We thought it best not to tell you guys about us until we knew it would really be forever. I thought it would have just been so awkward for you two if we'd broken up and then you have to keep seeing each other around campus," my mom explains.

"Yes, that would have been awkward," Nate says drily, and I know he's thinking that nothing could compare to my own awkwardness last night.

The waitress comes over with the bottle of champagne that Pierce ordered. Dom Perignon, I see as I look at the label. Woah, he must be loaded. *My new stepdad* must be loaded. She expertly pops the cork and pours us each an elegant flute, placing the bottle into a wine cooler next to the table.

Pierce takes his glass and raises it. "To a new family," he says, looking around the table. We all raise our glasses and clink them together. I manage to do so without making eye contact with Nate. The champagne tickles my throat on the way down. I've never wanted to drink a bottle of alcohol more in my entire life than at this moment, but I keep myself to a modest sip.

"So, honey, you told me you had some news, too?" my mom asks, as she puts down her glass.

"Oh, yes, though I don't think I can follow that announcement," I hedge with a smile.

"Please! You sounded excited on the phone," she encourages me.

"Well, I got a lawn room," I reveal. My mom gasps in excitement, but I see Pierce glance quickly at his son.

"I thought you said that they hadn't announced it yet," he says quietly.

"I…I knew you'd be disappointed. I was waitlisted. It was difficult, juggling two varsity sports, a double major—" Nate replies. I glance at my mom and then between the two men. Nate is looking down at the tablecloth.

"I was selected for a Lawn room, too," Pierce says, interrupting him and turning to me. "It's an important accomplishment."

"Thank you…" I say hesitantly. Nate looks so miserable. "Being waitlisted is impressive, too."

He glances up at me sharply, his eyes flashing. Shit. I heard it, too: pity.

"Well, congratulations, both of you," my mom breaks in. "I have no idea what I'm going to order! Everything looks so wonderful." She runs her finger down the menu in front of her. Having grown up in a family of Irish immigrants, my mom has always avoided conflict like the plague, though this time I'm glad for the change of subject.

I decide to order the steak since money doesn't seem to be an issue, and we each order a cocktail in addition to the champagne. Something begins to tug at the back of my brain after the waitress leaves to put in our food orders.

"Pierce, I'm sorry if this is an ignorant question, but were you in office? Your name sounds so familiar."

"Yes," he replies, looking pleased. "I'm a former congressman—"

"—For Virginia. Now I remember. You helped pass the campaign finance reforms." I smile.

"Good memory."

"One of my majors is Political Science, so I try to keep up with it."

"And your other major?"

"Global Health."

"You know, I run Thornhill and Co. Consulting of K Street, and we're still looking for a summer intern. Interested?"

"Dad, I thought you were going—" Nate breaks in before I can respond.

"And I thought you were going to get a Lawn Room," his dad replies, keeping his voice light. "So, Brynn, what do you think?"

"Well, um, I was just going to get a summer job back in Maryland to help pay for tuition," I murmur. Did Pierce promise his son the internship? I don't want to start off this relationship with Nate on the wrong foot.

"You don't need to worry about tuition now, honey," my mom says softly. I look at her in surprise.

Oh my god—is Pierce going to pay for my college bills? The thought hadn't even occurred to me. I look between them as they stare back at me calmly.

"Oh, oh, I didn't think—I mean, I'd love to, but I just—if Nate wants the—"

"Then it's settled," Pierce cuts in. "I tend to go into the office quite early, but we have an extra car you can use."

"Sorry? I don't understand."

"Well, Pierce and I are moving in together. I mean, I basically live there now, but I'm officially selling the old house, now that we're married."

"Right. Of course." My brain scrambles to process all the new information. Just as I'm working it all out, I feel a hand on my knee. I look down in surprise to see Nate's arm disappearing under the tablecloth. I glance at him. He's looking straight ahead as though nothing's happening. I struggle to maintain my composure as heat travels from his hand and all the way up to… "So, this summer, I'll be living with you then? All of you?"

Nate turns to smile at me politely. His hand moves another inch up the bare skin of my thigh. I widen my eyes at him but he doesn't react.

"That's right. We'll all be living at Pierce's house—"

"Our house," Pierce corrects my mom with a smile.

"*Our* house, in Potomac. It's got tons of space, beautiful views of the river. It'll be wonderful to have the summer to bond with each other, and really become a family."

Nate's hand moves another inch up my leg. I can feel the rough, calloused skin of his palm. I've never been so turned on in my life, but I'm struggling against it. What is he thinking? We're at dinner with our parents!

"I know you have some stuff at the old house, but we'll have it moved to the new one. Everything will be all set up when you get home," my mom says, smiling at me.

"Mmm," I reply, trying to focus on her words. "I wasn't that attached to the old place anyway," I add with a shrug. We'd moved a couple times after my dad left, so no one place has ever felt like home.

Nate's hand moves another inch up my thigh, pushing up the hem of my dress so his fingers rest under it. My whole body is tingling. Holy hell, I can barely breathe. I'm shocked Pierce and my mom don't seem to notice that anything's happening. With his other hand, Nate takes a calm sip from his champagne flute. Where's the waitress? He'll have to move his hand when the food comes.

He moves his hand up another inch. I can't take it any longer—another second and I'm going to start moaning. As my mom moves her head to Pierce's ear to murmur sweet nothings, I slide my fork off the table and press it tongs-first into the top of Nate's hand. I hear him make a sharp intake of breath and then his mouth twitches as he tries to hold position through the pain. I press down harder.

Suddenly he yanks his hand away and I just manage to stop my hand in time so the fork doesn't hit my leg. He turns to me and smiles, a wicked glimmer in his eyes.

He was fucking with me, I realize. That's his way of taking revenge for me showing him up in front of his dad? What a goddamn creep!

I lean toward him with a fake smile plastered on my face. "If you're that pissed about it, bring it up with your dad, don't take it out on me. I did *try* to turn it down." I hiss into his ear.

He turns to me with an equally fake smile. "I'll do whatever the hell I like, *Sis*." He says quietly so our parents can't hear.

The rest of the meal passes without Nate making another fake pass at me. The gears in my brain begin to move as I think about how I'm going to be spending the entire summer, and potentially many other seasons, living with this guy. My life has been completely upended tonight, and I need some time to process everything.

After the waitress clears our coffee cups and Pierce takes care of the bill *with a black Amex card*, we stand up to say goodbye. They're going to drive back to Maryland tonight since it takes under three hours. I hug Pierce goodbye, then my mom.

"I know this was a lot to take in, honey. We'll talk everything over, I promise," she whispers reassuringly, then kisses me on the cheek. I smile at her and begin to tear up—I'm pretty overwhelmed.

Nate surprises me by leaning in for a hug as our parents look on with a smile. "Great to meet you," he says, then whispers almost silently in my ear, "Sorry, we'll never get a chance to have that threesome, *Sis*."

I freeze as he pats my back once and then breaks away. He remembered. And now he will always know how attracted I am to him. I have a feeling I'm never going to hear the end of it.

CHAPTER FIVE

* * *

"I don't mean to question the relationship, it was just so sudden," I explain to my mom as she drives me home from the airport. I usually never fly to or from college, but Pierce insisted. My biggest worry was that Nate and I might be on the same flight, but luckily his exams ended earlier than mine. I want as much time as possible to prepare myself for our interactions.

"No, I get it, I really do," my mom assures me. "You can ask me anything about Pierce, or me and Pierce, and I won't be upset."

"He treats you well?"

"He's wonderful. He's always surprising me with little gifts, trips, even. I don't know what I've done to deserve him."

"Well, *I* think you're pretty great." I offer dramatically.

"Oh, I didn't mean it like that! I just mean, Pierce treats me like a princess. And the house is basically a castle," she adds, pointing to her right. I gasp at the flagstone mansion we're pulling alongside.

"Shut up. That's his house!? It's huge!"

"I know, right?" my mom replies with a laugh. "It has maid's quarters! But you'll get used to it, really."

"There's a *maid*?"

"He used to have a housekeeper/maid who would cook for him, but now I do most of that stuff. I love having someone else to cook for again. The maid just comes once a week now to do a really thorough cleaning," she explains as we pull through the wrought-iron gates leading the driveway.

"Are you still working at the salon?" She used to support herself as a manicurist at the tiny salon back in our small town in eastern Maryland.

"Nope, not anymore. I'm volunteering, though, and thinking of joining some charitable boards," she says nonchalantly. *My mom, a lady who lunches*, I think, shaking my head. I don't know if I can see it.

My mom presses a button on the car's dashboard and one of the two garage doors opens. We pull inside and I look around at the huge space as the door closes behind us. If I'm this in shock about the size of the garage, I can't imagine how I'll feel about the rest of the place.

After the tour, which took over an hour because the house is so massive, my mom finally leads me to my room. My head is swimming at the lavishness of my new home. As we walk down the plushly carpeted hallway, I'm alarmed to realize that I can actually *smell* Nate. He must be nearby somewhere. I've been dreading seeing him again and hoped I'd have more time to settle in before our first confrontation.

"Here's Nate's room," my mom says as we pass a partially open door. "He's out somewhere right now." I shake my head at myself. I wish I could turn off the part of my body that's attracted to him. If anything, though, my sex dreams about him have only become more frequent and more alarming ever since he laid his hand on my thigh. "And here's your room." I can't believe it's right next door to Nate's room. There are so many rooms in this place—I would have preferred to have a bit more separation between us.

"Whoa," I say as she pushes the door open, and my misgivings about the room are forgotten. A canopy with a delicate white fabric settled on it hangs over the four-poster bed in the center of the room. A matching nightstand, bureau, and vanity make up the rest of the furniture. The wallpaper is a tasteful, blue and white pattern with small birds on it that complements the light, airy feel of the room. I release the handle of my luggage and head over the to the window seat and kneel on it. There's a spectacular view of the Potomac River below—the house was clearly built to play up the amazing location. I glance to my left. "Is that my own bathroom?"

"Yup—no more sharing!" my mom replies gaily. I step inside and admire the all-white tile and huge tub. I've never been in a house so nice. I can't believe I'm actually going to call this place home from now on. "You want anything to eat?" my mom asks from the bedroom.

"Um, yeah, that would be great," I call over my shoulder.

"OK, I'll whip something up. You stay here and get settled. I'll be in the kitchen when you're ready to eat."

I wander back into the bedroom as my mom disappears down the stairs. There is one question I have that I can't bring myself to ask her. It's just…I know my mom worries about money, about me graduating from school with so much debt. It's not that I think she would have married Pierce just for the money, but I worry that it might have clouded her judgment a bit. They got married so quickly—can she really know him that well?

Maybe I'm just falling back into my usual pattern of co-dependency and mothering *her*. She's a grown woman, I can't control what she does and I'm not responsible for her decisions…not to mention, I *am* hugely relieved to not have to carry around student loans for the rest of my life.

I kick my sandals off and sink back down onto the window seat. The Potomac is a dark green sliver barely visible through the bushy trees that line the back of the estate and continue down to the shoreline. I startle as a figure breaks the stillness. I recognize Nate's head as he walks up from the lower lawn to the pool, a lacrosse stick tucked over his shoulder. Sheesh—is he training already? School just ended!

I bite my lip as I watch him toss the stick on the deck and peel off his shirt. He uses it to wipe the sweat off his face, then tosses it on a chair and kicks off his sneakers. His body is just…impossible. I mean, I guess it makes sense. Two varsity sports are probably enough to give anyone a body like a Greek god, but he also has the face to match.

He jumps in the pool and I watch him swim a lap, the cool blue water cascading over his muscular back and shoulders. I need to get used to seeing him like this—and stop acting like a total freak every time we're in the same room. This is my new normal.

"Your food's ready!" my mom calls upstairs, her voice echoing a bit in the multi-level foyer. I jump up and head downstairs. I turn into a formal dining room before finding my way to the kitchen. I stop as I realize the kitchen windows look directly out onto the pool. Great. "I can't believe Nate's already in the pool. The water's still freezing," my mom comments.

"Yeah, he's crazy…" I reply, before I really hear what she said. I'm too distracted by Nate's backstroke, his arms cutting cleanly through the water.

"So you two never once ran into each other on campus in the three years you've been at UVA?" she asks, sliding a BLT onto the glass table in the breakfast nook. We sit down across from each other and I start eating.

"No, well…we hadn't ever *met*."

"But?" my mom digs, hearing a slight hesitation in my voice.

"Well, Nate's really well known around campus. He starts on the lacrosse and crew teams, he's smart, good—" I catch myself and pretend to clear my throat.

"Good-looking?" My mom asks with a smile.

"Mom…" I groan.

"Well, he is. I'm not blind. Actually, Pierce looked just like him when he was his age." I see Nate get out of the pool over my mom's shoulder and shake himself off. I force myself to look down at my sandwich as he walks across to a lawn chair and lies down.

"What happened to Nate's mom?"

My mom winces. "Pierce doesn't really like to talk about it—too painful. Apparently, she cheated on him and then abandoned him and Nate. They never see her."

"Oh, that's awful," I murmur, trying to shove down the twinge of pity I feel for my new stepbrother.

"I think it's one of the things that brought us together—raising a child by ourselves."

My eyes flick to the door as Nate slides it open. He's put his shirt back on but it clings to his still damp torso, emphasizing his muscular pecs and shoulders. He drops his sneakers on the mat as he shuts the door behind him.

"Hey Nate," my mom greets him. "Would you like a sandwich?"

"You don't have to do that," he says, a little gruffly.

"I don't mind at all," she replies, standing to move back to the counter. He pauses, then sits in her abandoned chair a bit reluctantly. "It's so funny that you and Brynn never met at school!"

"I think there might have been one time—" he says, glancing at me, that same devilish look back in his eyes. I feel his knee come to rest against mine under the table, and I quickly cross my legs.

"In class. We have been in a few of the same classes together," I clarify, narrowing my eyes at him.

"We have?" he asks looking genuinely surprised. My mom quietly spreads mayo on a slice of bread at the marble island.

"Yes," I whisper, embarrassed. Of course he wouldn't remember all of the times we've sat in the same classroom—only the time when I ogled him in the doorway of his bedroom and completely embarrassed myself. I blush. I want to sink into this seat cushion and disappear. He frowns at me then turns his palm over and begins to pick at a callous.

"So honey, Pierce says you'll start your internship on Monday, OK? That'll give you a few days to settle in," my mom says as she slides the sandwich in front of Nate.

"Sounds good," I reply, glancing at Nate out of the corner of my eye.

"I'm having someone over for dinner tomorrow night," he announces rather abruptly.

"Oh, wonderful. A friend from around here?"

"Not a friend, really. A girl I dated in high school," Nate clarifies. I keep my eyes trained carefully forward.

"Do you know if she has any dietary restrictions?" my mom asks, excitedly flying into hostess mode. "I could make this chicken dish my mom passed down, or…"

I tune out as she offers more ideas, and polish off my sandwich as quickly as possible so I can excuse myself and go upstairs. I sigh as I close my bedroom door behind me. So now I have to have dinner with

Nate's ex-girlfriend. Is this what the rest of the summer is going to be like? Nate punishing me for his father's favor by exploiting my attraction to him? I'd rather be back in the library, buried in a book.

CHAPTER SIX

* * *

I push the sautéed chicken around my plate as I try not to watch Nate drape his arm around the back of Dana's chair. She's pretty. Very pretty. And sweet. I wish she weren't so sweet so I could hate her for a good reason.

"So how long did you two date?" my mom asks.

"Well, it was on and off, so…hard to say. He actually went to prom with one of my friends," she replies, jokingly nudging Nate, who at least has the grace to blush.

"Nate…" his dad says, shaking his head admonishingly.

"Oh, it's OK. I went with one of his friends," Dana says with a smile. "I think we both knew it wasn't meant to be."

"A couple of my friends met their husbands in high school," my mom says, resting her fork on her plate. "Though I read an article recently that said that twenty-eight percent of women meet their husbands in college." She looks pointedly at me and I jump up.

"I'll clear," I announce. I have a feeling I know where this conversation is headed and I want to avoid it.

"Oh, thank you, Brynn," Pierce says, as I stack the plates on top of one another.

"No problem," I reply. "I waited tables in high school."

"Same," Nate says, as I reach in front of him to take his plate.

"You did not," I retort, before I can think. He looks up at me and raises his eyebrows, his gaze unreadable beneath them.

Pierce laughs. "It's true."

"My dad says working is the only way to build character," Nate reports quietly.

"Oh," I say, blushing as I push my way through the swinging door into the kitchen. I place the china carefully next to the sink and lean onto the counter.

God, I feel like I can't say anything right around Nate. My mind freezes up while my body is set on fire.

"So, are you dating anyone at school, Brynn?" Pierce asks. Damn him.

"Not right now," I reply, sitting back down.

"Who were you dating? Maybe I know him," Nate says, his dark eyes picking up the candlelight in the table's elaborate centerpiece. My mom spent all afternoon on it.

"Probably not," I say evasively, pasting a polite smile on my face. He really knows how to get under my skin. The truth is, I've never really dated anyone, much as my mom pushes me, and as much as I'm embarrassed by the fact. "Who wants dessert?"

I manage to sidestep any more questioning by bringing out the last course, though now I'm starting to think about the fact that Nate and Dana are probably going to want to go off somewhere after this and have sex. I hope it's not in Nate's room. What if I can hear them through the wall?

My mom insists on clearing the dessert plates, and Nate and Dana stand up. Pierce and Nate start talking quietly, and Dana comes over to me.

"You are so gorgeous." She offers. "I have to ask: what do you use on your skin?"

"I—what? Um, soap?" Oh man, she really makes it difficult to hate her.

"Soap? Just…soap? Oh my god, I have this whole routine," she says, laughing at herself.

"Well, thanks. I guess I'll be seeing you around often?" I ask, but she looks surprised. "Because you and Nate are dating."

"We're not really dating," she confides to me. "He's not the type, and I gave up hope years ago. But just look at him—can you blame me for coming back?" she says with a grin, then her eyes widen. "Oh my gosh—sorry! I forgot for a second that he's your brother!"

"*Step*-brother," I correct her. "Well, I'm gonna head upstairs. It was really nice to meet you, Dana."

"You, too," she replies, stepping away to join Pierce and Nate's conversation. I head into the foyer but at the last second decide not to go upstairs. I need some air. I find myself heading down the hallway and to the French doors in the wood-paneled study. They open onto the patio and I step outside with relief, closing the door behind me.

The firm breeze from the river calls me forward and I head down toward it. I circle around the swimming pool on the first level of the backyard, and then down to a grassy lawn with a lacrosse goal set up on one end. The wooden stairs down to the rocky beach are set on the right side, and it takes me a minute to find them in the dark.

As I head down the steps, I see the Potomac spread out in front of me. The water rushes hungrily by, lit only by the sparsely set houses on the cliffs surrounding it. As I step onto the shore, I can feel the rocks pressing up through my sandals, and boulders casting long, dark shadows on either side of me. This is no white-sand beach. The river runs dangerously fast after rains, and there are even white-water rapids along parts of it.

I look back at the steps behind me and then back out at the river. I feel so out of place here. Even though our old house didn't really feel like home either, I wish I were there now, stretched out on the ratty old couch, with my mom in her chair, watching something on our small TV. I don't know if I'll ever be able to feel like I belong here. I'll always feel like a guest in Pierce's house.

I walk down closer to the water until I can feel the pebbles getting smaller underneath my feet. I don't want my shoes to get wet. I jump as a bird breaks out of a tree above me. I can just see it as it flies off, its body a moving ink blot against the dark sky.

I wish I could follow it.

I turn and walk back toward the steps, feeling as lonely as I've ever felt. I shake my head at myself as I climb the wooden stairs. My mom is happy, and I'm fortunate to live in a place like this. *Stop feeling sorry for yourself, Brynn.*

As I walk across the lower lawn, I look up and see my mom and Pierce's bedroom light go off. I guess they're turning in early tonight. I walk up toward the pool and freeze as I hear a moan. The lights downstairs are all off except one in the hall, and the pool's lights underneath the water. My eyes dart around and fall on two writhing bodies on a poolside lounge chair. Nate and Dana.

I stare as Nate whips off his own shirt and then Dana's. I know I should move but I don't. The blue pool lights shimmer against his back muscles as he expertly undoes Dana's bra and pulls off her pants and underwear.

Leave, you pervert! my brain commands me, but my body stays firmly glued in place, even as it throbs with desire. One of Nate's hands massages Dana's ample breasts, and the other disappears beneath her. Dana cries out immediately and I almost gasp myself, as though his hands are moving against me. I can practically feel his touch on me, his hot breath against my ear as his expert fingers move inside me…

Nate grunts and pushes against her. She struggles to contain herself as he thrusts slowly in and out of her. *Oh my god—what am I doing!?* I step back with a jolt as though I'm breaking out of a trance and almost trip over the hydrangea bush next to me in my hurry to get away. I run as quickly and quietly as I can around the side of the house and to the front. I reach the front door and pray that Nate is going to lock up later. I feel the doorknob turn and push the door open in relief. I hurry up the curving staircase and down the hall into my room, kicking off my sandals before hurling myself onto my bed and burying my head in the pillows.

I can feel my cheeks burning with mortification over what I just witnessed and the uncontrollable desire I felt. I've had crushes before, but none like my obsession with Nate. And even after finally meeting him, only to have him tease me and push my buttons, I still feel so physically drawn to him.

I pull my face out of the pillow and crawl to the nightstand, pulling my dog-eared copy of *Lady Chatterley's Lover* out of the top drawer. Just as I'm opening it to the folded-over page, there's a quiet knock at my door. I toss my book on the bed and walk to it, hoping and praying it's not Nate.

I almost jump as I pull open the door and Nate's face appears, shrouded in the darkness of the hallway. He leans forward, leaning his forearm on the doorjamb as I step back nervously. His wavy hair looks particularly unruly, and his lips are curved in a slight smile.

"Technically speaking, does a Peeping Tom have to be outside, looking inside? Or does the term still apply if both, or all three, parties are outdoors?" he asks, calmly, tilting his chin up slightly as he considers me.

"I…I don't…" I stammer, feeling heat crawl up the back of my neck.

"You. Were. Watching us," he accuses me, narrowing his eyes.

"I'm sorry. I didn't mean to. I just…I was down at the river…how did you…?"

"I heard a twig snap and saw you running away like a drunken ostrich."

"Did Dana—?"

"No, and I didn't tell her."

"Thank god."

"So? What did you think?" He smirks.

"Oh, I'm so sorry, again. I'm so embarrassed," I rush on. It strikes me that this is the longest conversation I've ever had with my new stepbrother. And it's about how I'm a pervert. Fantastic.

"*Why* were you watching us?" he asks, stepping forward into my room. I take another step away from him.

"Um, I...I don't know. It just sort of happened. I didn't mean to."

"Liar," he comments lightly.

"Asshole." It slips out before I can stop myself.

He tilts his head slightly. "Prude," he levels at me. I look down. Maybe I am a prude, but I don't want to be. "What's that?" he asks. When I look back up at him, I see him gazing past me, to my book on the bed.

"Nothing, just a book," I say, but he's breezing past me toward it. I hurry after him but he reaches the bed before me and picks up the book. "See?" I say defiantly.

"I know what *Lady Chatterley's Lover* is about," he says, looking at me with a smug grin. Shit. "Maybe not such a prude after all," he adds, running his eyes up and down my body. I swallow hard. "You know what I think?" he asks, stepping toward me. I step away again, feeling one of the posts of my bed against my back. "I think you want me. I think you can barely contain yourself."

"That's mighty arrogant of you," I comment. I begin to tug the ends of my hair nervously.

"Why are you doing that?" He asks, frowning.

"It's just a nervous habit," I say with a shrug, and drop my hand.

"So I make you nervous?"

"No," I reply quickly. "Just you being in here…"

"I'm only arrogant if I'm wrong."

"Wrong about what?" I feel the urge to pull my hair again but don't want to give him the satisfaction.

"Wrong about you wanting me. Let's give it a test—" he narrows his eyebrows, studying me. "I'm going to kiss you now, and all you have to do is tell me to stop."

"What? That's crazy. Not to mention you just fucked Dana, and now you expect me to kiss you?" I protest, but he steps toward me. I try to pull backward but I'm already pressed against my bedpost. Desire unfurls deep in my stomach as his eyes lock onto mine.

"If it's crazy, just tell me to stop," he whispers teasingly, and moves closer. His musky scent fills my nose and my mind begins to swim. I feel wetness trickling down my thigh as he curls his arms around me, grasping the bedpost with both hands behind my lower back. He's so close to me. I can feel heat radiating off him. His legs and chest sink against me and he moves his lips toward mine. Just a few inches between Nate Thornhill's mouth and mine. Now an inch. Now two centimeters…I can feel his warm breath against my partially open lips…

"Stop." I whisper.

He freezes but doesn't pull away, as though he can't believe what he's just heard. Though truthfully, I'm marveling at my own restraint. I can feel his erection against my thigh—I know he wants me, too.

Now I can beat him at his own game. I lean forward slightly, allowing my lips to brush against his as I speak, "Unless *you* don't want to."

His eyes, which were focused on my lips, flick back up to meet mine. I force myself to stay steady even as I'm consumed by the lust in his gaze. He stares at me for a moment, then pushes off the bedpost and steps back. He opens his mouth, about to say something, but nothing comes out. I remain pressed against the bedpost as he turns and moves toward the door. Without looking back, he shuts it behind him.

I stumble forward and take a deep breath. It's like he takes all the air out of the room and I can't breathe when he's around.

I can't believe I just rejected him. I'm stunned, but I also feel like giving myself a standing ovation. I just resisted the advances of Nate Thornhill, my fantasy of almost three years. I should win a willpower award. I knew that if I'd let him kiss me, I would forever lose any kind of power in our relationship. I'd be just be another pathetic girl who fell for his charms.

Of course, the downside is that I'm more turned on than I've ever been in my life, and I'm alone with a book again. I sigh and crawl back onto my bed. I have a feeling that whatever is happening between me and my stepbrother, I haven't seen the end of it yet.

CHAPTER SEVEN

* * *

"I'm so happy there's another girl working here!" Constance says, swiveling around on her desk chair. She's my new cubicle mate, and one of only a handful of other interns at Thornhill and Co.

"Ah, there. My Outlook is finally working," I announce, opening the email system on my desktop.

"So they'll want you to sign an NDA and stuff, but after, want to go to lunch?" she asks.

"What's an NDA?" I turn to face her.

"Non-disclosure agreement. There are a ton of Senators and big business types who come in here, and you can't tell *anyone*. Very important," she says in hushed tones. She seems very pleased that she's snagged this coveted internship, which is probably why I haven't told her that I'm the boss's stepdaughter. I've never benefited from nepotism before, and it feels strange and uncomfortable to me now.

"Oh. Well I'd love to get lunch later this week, but I'm having lunch with my friend Allison today. We go to UVA together, and she's got an internship at this urban planning place in Georgetown, so I'm going to meet up with her."

"Cool. Georgetown has really good shopping. I'd love to go with you sometime. Fashion is like, my side hobby, and you have a stylist's dream body."

"I don't think I—" I begin my canned response to a shopping invitation before I realize that maybe I *can* afford it. And Constance looks so perfectly chic in her patterned cardigan and statement necklace. "You know, that would be wonderful. I really don't know what to buy."

"Oh, I can help you with that. But careful not to wear anything too tight around Mr. Thornhill," she adds, rolling her eyes.

"What do you mean?" I ask with a frown.

"Oh my god, who is *that*?" Constance asks, breaking away from our conversation to stand and peer over our cubicle wall. I join her to see Nate and

Pierce walking down the hallway together toward the elevator bank. They must be having lunch together.

"That's his son," I reply, immediately sitting down again.

"He looks like a Polo model!" Constance exclaims, sitting back down.

"Um, what were you saying about Pierce—Mr. Thornhill—just then?"

"Well, I've never had an issue, but maybe he's just not into Asian girls," she says, throwing her black hair over her shoulder carelessly. "From what I've heard, though, he has a certain reputation."

"Oh, no," I reply, worriedly tugging on my hair. Shit. Shit. I knew he was too good to be true.

"Don't worry. From what I've heard, he's pretty harmless, he's just from a different generation when it comes to women around the office—especially young women," she adds.

"Mmhm," I reply, my mind already spiraling into crisis mode.

"You OK, Brynn?"

"Maybe he's changed, though. I mean, he's married now," I say, clinging to a speck of hope.

"Yeah, I heard he got married." She shrugs. "Could be. I don't think it's something that's been really recent or anything."

I nod, feeling slightly mollified. We both spin back to our computers as we hear footsteps approaching our cubicle. I glance up to see Pierce and Nate appear in the opening.

"Brynn, this is going to sound awful," Pierce begins, and I brace myself. "But Nate and I had plans to go to lunch, and we got down to the lobby before I realized how rude it was not to invite you along."

Phew. For a second I thought he overheard our conversation. "Oh, that's so nice, but I actually have lunch plans with my best friend from school, anyway."

"Oh I see…well, enjoy! There are some great restaurants around here. We just wanted to let you know you were invited," Pierce says kindly, though from Nate's frown I'm guessing that it was more his idea than his son's. "Constance, right?" he says, turning to her.

"Yes, that's right," she squeaks.

"Alright, well, we better get going or we'll be late for our reservation. See you at home!" Pierce says with a wave, and walks off with Nate in tow. Huh. I notice that Nate didn't say a single word to me. I guess he doesn't like being the one left wanting for once.

"Why will Mr. Thornhill see you at home?" Constance says, slowly turning her desk chair to face me, a weird expression on her face.

"Um, well, I'm his stepdaughter. He just married my mom."

Constance gasps and buries her face in her hands. "Oh my god, oh my god, I'm so fired. I'm fired, right?"

"What? No! I don't have that kind of authority, I'm just an intern, like you."

"You're the boss's daughter, and I was just gossiping about him!"

"*Step*-daughter, and I get it. If I'd heard rumors like that, I might want to warn other women I work with, too."

"But I don't even know if they're true, I'm so sorry," she says miserably.

"Really, it's OK. And I'm sorry that I didn't tell you earlier that I'm his stepdaughter. I just…you know, didn't want it to seem like it was the only reason I got the internship. I mean, I really do work very hard."

"Of course you do! Of course. Yes. I should get back to work," Constance says, turning to her computer and beginning to type rapidly.

* * *

"…And now I'm worried she's going to keep acting really weird around me," I confide to Allison over a Caesar salad at Clyde's on M Street.

"Do you think it's true?" she whispers, leaning over the table between us.

"I don't know…I mean, maybe he was just a flirt, and it got blown out of proportion, you know?"

"I bet that's what it is," Allison says, nodding her head sagely. "Who knows how stories like that really get started? And once they're out there, you can't erase them."

"I hope that's what it is…I don't want to discount some woman's, or women's, experience just because it would be inconvenient for me, though, and painful for my mom. She would be so crushed if it were true."

"I wouldn't worry about it. And that girl said they were old stories, right?"

"Right."

"And you said he treats your mom well, so I bet they're just ugly rumors."

"Yeah, yeah," I reply, pushing the thought of Pierce's alleged misbehavior to the back of my brain. "How's the place you're staying at George Washington?" I ask, knowing she's taking advantage of a program at the nearby university to give summer interns a low-cost place to stay in an otherwise expensive city.

"It's fine. My roommate's kinda loud, though. How's your new house?"

"It's so big! I don't know why anyone would need that much space. I mean before my mom and I got there, it was just for two people. Well, three, including the maid."

"There's a maid?!"

"There was. She doesn't live there anymore. Oh, and there's all this flagstone on it, so I thought it was old, but my mom said that Pierce had the house built around fifteen years ago. He must have spent a lot of money to make something so new look worn-in."

"You're lucky," Allison says.

"I know."

"How's the stepbrother? I don't know if I could live with a dumb jock."

"Well, Nate's not dumb. I've been in a few classes with him, and he's really smart. He was even waitlisted for a Lawn Room."

"You're a little defensive of him," Allison observes, sipping her water.

"Yeah, I guess so. I don't know why though. He's been playing these weird mind games with me."

"Mind games?" she repeats, frowning. I push a crouton around my plate as I think about how much to tell her. I have a feeling it's not the kind of situation she'd condone, but I also really want to talk to someone about what's been going on.

"Well, you remember that I used to have a crush on him?"

"Yeah, I remember you saying something about it sophomore year."

"I…I *still* have a crush on him. Or I think I do…I don't know. I'm definitely attracted to him, and he's aware of the fact. He can be really rude, and then last night, he almost kissed me, but he…"

"Woah, what? I mean, Brynn, he's your stepbrother."

"I know! But only for the last few weeks, and—"

"OK…but what if you *did* kiss? What then? You'd have to see him every day, because your mom and his dad are *married*. And then even if you weren't living together, what about holidays? You'd be cutting the Thanksgiving turkey and sitting across from the guy you'd made out with…for *every* Thanksgiving."

"Ugh, you're right," I reply, dropping my fork and covering my face with my hands. This is why I didn't want to tell Allison—she'd throw logic in the face of my hormones. But the truth is, she's right. I feel like a bucket of cold water has just been poured over my head. "You're right," I repeat. "I can't believe I even let it get this far."

I head back to the office after lunch and spend the rest of the afternoon sitting in an awkward silence with Constance. I try to get her to engage about online shopping, but she only offers me one-word responses. Later in the day I meet another intern named Greg, a cute, strawberry-blonde guy who blushes when I look him in the eye. He is more the kind of person I should be looking to date. I just wish I felt that same rush that I do whenever I'm around Nate.

I drive home just after six in the old Audi that was just sitting in the Thornhill's garage. It's definitely the most expensive car I've ever driven, and it's fun to really let out the engine on the short stretch of the Beltway on my way back to Potomac. I park in the garage and let myself in to the small anteroom off the kitchen, where I kick off my shoes.

"Mom?" I call out, before spotting her outside on the back lawn, talking on the phone as the sun sets behind her. I head upstairs with my tote bag still over my shoulder. The huge house is silent as I walk up the steps and down the hallway. Nate must still be at his internship. My mom told me he got one at some think tank downtown.

I drop my bag as I walk into my bedroom and push the door almost closed behind me with my foot. I can't wait to get this skirt off. It's my one pencil skirt, and it's a little itchy around my waist.

I step into the bathroom and turn on the elegant faucet in the sink. I tie my hair behind my head with a loose elastic and splash some cool water on my skin. First days are always exhausting, but I think today was unusually so. As I look back up to my reflection, dripping with water, I see something move in the mirror. I stare at it blankly, not understanding what I'm seeing. The mirror above the sink is reflecting the mirror above my vanity in the bedroom, which is in turn reflecting an image from my partially open bedroom door. It's Nate, I realize. He's standing outside my door, and he doesn't realize I can see him.

I look down at the sink, pretending to watch the last of the water as it swirls down the drain. A shiver of excitement runs through me at the idea that Nate could actually be interested in me—I mean, he's there, right now, watching me. Before I process what I'm doing, before I can think of all the reasons not to, I slowly move my hands to my lower back and undo the clasp at the top of the zipper, then unzip my skirt. I let it fall in a pile at my feet, then step out of it. I look up carefully and Nate is still there in the double reflection.

Allison's warning echoes through my mind but I keep going. I feel high, high on the feeling that I'm actually desired. I catch hold of the back of my rather shapeless blouse in my hands and pull it up over my head, then toss it onto the floor. As I look back in the mirror, I try to imagine what someone else might see when they look at me, without my constant negative interior monologue telling me nasty things about myself. Do I have the kind of body that someone like Nate could find attractive?

Now down to my bra and underwear, I begin to feel nervous, but I reach up to unclasp my bra. I feel the straps loosen on my shoulders and bring my hands forward to catch it as it falls.

"Brynn? You home?" I hear my mom call from the foyer. I freeze, holding the bra against my breasts. I glance up. Nate is gone.

"Yup, I'm home!" I yell back.

"I saw your shoes! I'm coming up—I want to hear all about your first day." I hear her footsteps on the staircase and hurriedly refasten my bra. Nothing like your mom's voice to kill your libido.

CHAPTER EIGHT

* * *

The next couple weeks of my new life seem to pass rather quickly, mostly due to the fact that Nate is always out with his friends after work, and our run-ins have been few and far between. I've settled into a routine of sorts, even if I still don't feel like I'm at home here.

I'd gone to bed early last night, with the intention of sleeping in this morning before visiting museums with Allison later in the day. However a loud noise from downstairs awakens me—I stare bleary eyed at my alarm clock, it's only 6:15am. Who'd be awake this early on a Saturday morning?

I get out of bed and tiptoe to my door. I open it a little and hear something shuffling around downstairs. I tiptoe out into the hallway and see everyone's bedroom doors are closed. I know there's an alarm system—I had to memorize the passcode. Maybe an ungainly mouse is exploring? I creep down the staircase and through the dining room. The noises sounded like they were coming from the kitchen. The swinging door is open, and I peak my head around it, my heartbeat blasting in my ears.

Suddenly, Nate steps out in front of me.

"Fuck!" he exclaims, and I jump back, startled.

"Oh, god, I thought you were a burglar."

"Then you should have called 911," he retorts brusquely, turning his back to me and walking to the island.

"Well, you should be glad I didn't." Sheesh, does he have to find something wrong with everything I say? "What are you doing up so early anyway?"

"I was just working out."

"Wow. This early?" I ask, moving around him. He's fiddling with something in front of him.

"Yeah, every morning. I need to stay in shape during the off-season."

"I'd be exhausted if—" I break off, as I see blood dripping from his palms onto the granite countertop. "Oh my god, you're bleeding!" I gasp.

"Yeah, I just can't get this fucking tape to…" he struggles to wind a bandage around his palm.

"Let me," I say, spying a first aid kit on the counter by the window. From the blood smeared on it, I can see Nate's already gone through it.

"You don't have to," he protests.

"Come over here. The light's better," I instruct him.

"Do you know what you're doing?" he asks, less than thrilled to accept my help.

"More than you," I reply with a smile, nodding at the mess of tape around his palm. I wash my hands in the sink and then open up the kit. I take a pair of surgical scissors and cut off the tape that he's already applied. I glance up slightly, and for the first time it hits me that he's shirtless, wearing only a pair of gym shorts and sneakers. He's covered in sweat. "How'd this happen?"

"I over-trained a little. Got dizzy, tripped on a rock and held out my hands to break my fall," he replies, eyes downcast as he watches me work.

"Over-training for what? Lacrosse or crew?" I ask as I pull out a piece of gauze and a bottle of hydrogen peroxide.

"Both. Either," he murmurs.

"This is going to sting," I warn him, as I pat the gashes on his hands with the soaked gauze. He hisses slightly as the liquid stings him, but doesn't move. I slide my other hand under his, to stabilize it as I cleanse the wound of dirt. I've never touched him this long before. "Other hand." He switches hands and I go to work cleaning the other one. "Maybe you should take a little time off from training," I suggest quietly.

"Or I could just work out my leg muscles," he says, and I look up to see a wry grin on his face.

"Mmm," I murmur, smiling too. "You know," I go on, a bit more bravely, "I heard that only one varsity athlete got a Lawn Room, because sports are such a time commitment, much less a two-sport athlete—"

"Don't do that," he grunts. "I don't want your pity."

"It's not pity, it's facts."

"I was born with everything, I have no excuse for not achieving my all of goals."

"Where did you hear that? It sounds like—" I break off, feeling him stiffen under my touch. I was going to say *his father* but I can tell he doesn't want me to go there. "You're just really hard on yourself, that's all," I say instead. I gently dab some Neosporin onto the cuts.

"I know what everyone sees when they look at me," he replies quietly. "Entitled…born with a silver spoon in my mouth…I work as hard as I do so that no one can say I succeed because of my family's wealth."

I frown. That's half of the equation I think, but it seems like he doesn't see how hard his father pushes him.

"I got a little bit of that at work the other day," I say, wondering if it's OK to broach the topic of the internship he wanted. I take a dry piece of gauze and cover his palm with it before picking up the tape and beginning to wrap it around his hand. "When they found out I was Pierce's stepdaughter, I mean. Feels weird."

"Your first experience of nepotism?"

"Yeah," I say with a smile. "Actually, my mom once got me a part-time job as the receptionist at the salon where she used to work, so I guess that's not true."

"Where does your dad work?"

"No idea. Probably a repair shop somewhere. He's a mechanic, or he was. Last time we heard from him was several years ago. He was in Florida then, but he never stays in one place very long."

"So you're the first in your family to go to college," he observes, as I finish taping one hand and move to the other.

"Yep."

"Is that why you're so serious?"

"Am I?" I ask, my eyes moving up to his.

"Serious isn't the right word…distant, maybe."

"Distant? That's worse," I reply, feeling a little hurt.

"I didn't mean to insult you. I'm just trying to figure you out. We were really in class together? Which one?"

"There were three. The first was this American History survey class freshman year."

"Professor Michaels?"

"Yeah. I always sat behind you, though. I'm not surprised you didn't see me," I say, pressing down slightly as I finish wrapping his hands.

"I am," he replies. I glance up sharply, but his eyes aren't focused on my face. They're looking at my body, which I now realize is quite exposed in my thin, white cotton nightie. I completely forgot I was wearing it. There's a moment of silence, and I suddenly become very aware of every inch of myself, and every inch of him. His smell of sweat, beads of it still dripping forward down his chest, through a smattering of hair between his nipples. Allison's face appears in my mind, and I'm reminded of what she said.

"I'm done."

"What?" he says, his eyes pulling up to mine.

"With your hands. I'm done."

"Right."

I grab a glass from the cabinet and pour him some water from the faucet. "Here, you felt dizzy because you're dehydrated."

"Thanks," he says. He reaches for the glass with his left hand, which is closer, and then pauses and takes it awkwardly with his right.

"What was that?" I ask, frowning.

"What?"

"Let me see your left arm," I reply, reaching for him, but he pulls back.

"No, no, it's nothing."

"What is?"

"My shoulder. It's just a little tendonitis."

"Oh really? Did a doctor tell you that?"

"Not exactly."

"WebMD?" I ask, raising my eyebrows. He shrugs, then winces. "You need to take better care of yourself. You can't keep pushing yourself so hard." He frowns, and doesn't respond. "Well, at least take some Tylenol for the pain," I add as I pour two pills into my hand and begin to repack the first aid kit with the other.

"That's OK."

I tilt my head at him. "Pain isn't going to make you heal any faster," I point out.

"Fine," he says with a little smile. I blush as his fingertips scrape my palm as he takes the pills.

"Well. I think I'm going back to bed. I'm supposed to check out some of the Smithsonian museums later, so…" I trail off, feeling awkward now.

"OK, see you later," he says, turning toward the back door. I pause for a moment, then head back toward the staircase. Just like that, the one real conversation that my stepbrother and I have ever had is over. I could practically feel him closing back up at the end there. I climb the steps and shut my bedroom door behind me. I feel more confused now than ever about our relationship. I didn't think it could get any weirder after that peep show I gave him, but somehow this candid glimpse of him makes things even more complicated.

I close my eyes and try to fall back to sleep, but when my alarm goes off at ten, I'm still wide awake.

CHAPTER NINE

*** * * ***

The humidity is really starting to thicken by the middle of June, and it's a wonder that I haven't taken advantage of our pool yet. The only swimsuit I have is an old athletic one-piece, and I pull it on reluctantly in my bedroom. My mom keeps asking me if I want to go shopping, but I haven't taken her up on it yet. All her new clothes look wonderful but I think I'd feel uncomfortable spending so much money on myself.

I head down the hallway and almost bump into Nate as he leaves his bedroom. I reflexively cross my hands over my chest, even though I know he's seen me in less.

"Hey," I say.

"Hey," he replies. It's the same conversation we've had ever since I saw him in the kitchen that morning. We quickly slipped into polite, but formal, interactions with each other afterward. If I had to choose between this and the mind games we started out with, I might choose the mind games.

The doorbell rings and I start to move past him to answer it.

"It's OK I'll get it. It's my friend Jackson." He walks down the hallway toward the stairs.

I follow after him, and turn toward the backyard once we're in the foyer. I hear his friend walk in just as I exit the French doors. There's a chest set against the house with the outdoor towels in it, so I grab one and set it on a chair.

The area around the pool it is paved with light stones before it turns into grass, and lounge chairs and a table with an umbrella are carefully set around it. I turn to the pool and step gingerly onto the first step in the shallow end. It's nice—warm, but still refreshing in the hot summer day. I step down the rest of the way until the water circles around my stomach, and then dive forward. I swim to the other end, where the water gets darker and deeper, then push off and glide onto my back. I open my eyes as I push the water past me with my hands and look up toward the house rising against the sun on my left.

A flash of movement in the second floor window grabs my attention. There's a figure moving there, pulling a curtain aside. At first I think it's Nate—it's his room, I think—but then I catch a glimpse of blonde hair. Must be his friend Jackson. I turn onto my stomach and dive back under the water. I want Nate to be the one watching me.

I was never much into sports, but I've always wondered if I'd be any good at them. I push harder for the last couple laps and finally pull my head up at the shallow end, gasping for breath. I take the steps back out of the pool and walk around to my towel and dry off my hair, then drape it onto the chair and lay down on it. I can feel the suit clinging to my torso, and water sitting in my belly button. I hear the door to the house open behind me and shield my eyes from the sun as I turn around to see who it is.

Jackson bounds out of the door, his face spread in a genial grin. "Hey, you must be Brynn. I'm Jackson, one of Nate's oldest friends."

"Nice to meet you," I say as we shake hands. I notice Nate lagging behind, standing just outside the door and looking reluctant to put another foot toward the pool.

"Come on, man, let's get in. I've been dreaming about this pool for days."

"We shouldn't bother her, she likes to be alone," Nate says reluctantly. Jackson pulls off his shirt, and I look down at my interlaced fingers in my lap. He's got a great body. Maybe not as good as Nate's, but whose is? Jackson kicks off his flip-flops and jumps in, his splash narrowly missing me. Nate slowly walks toward the chair furthest from me, and takes off his shirt. I watch his back muscles tense as he lifts it off his head.

"Nate and I grew up playing lacrosse together," Jackson says, swimming to the edge of the pool and leaning his elbows onto the deck in front of me.

"Hm? Oh," I reply, as Nate dives in the deep end.

"So you guys go to school together?"

"Yup. UVA—I mean, of course you knew that."

"Which sorority are you in?" he asks, pushing his wet hair out of his eyes.

"I'm not. It's expensive, and I'm already pretty busy with work. Um, where do you go?"

Nate pops up next to Jackson. They make quite a pair, Nate with his dark eyes and Jackson with his light blonde locks.

"You wanna get some food now?" Nate asks.

"Dude we just got here. Besides, you're not supposed to eat for thirty minutes after you swim."

"Before," Nate and I both chime in. We glance at each other as he continues. "You're not supposed to eat for thirty minutes *before.* Why wouldn't it be OK to eat after you swim?"

"I dunno," Jackson replies, flashing me a blindingly white smile. "Just thought that was the rule." I find myself smiling back at him. He has a boyish charm that's infectious.

"I'm pretty sure that's a myth adults made up so they'd have time to eat their own lunch without the kids swimming unsupervised." I smile.

"Ah that makes more sense. You grow up around here?" he asks me.

"Yeah, on the Eastern shore."

"Oh, sweet. My family has a vacation house there. I love going out there. Sailing in the bay and everything. You go sailing a lot?"

"Um, not really," I reply. Nate kicks off the wall and begins to swim back and forth behind Jackson. I guess he's decided not to take it easy on his injured shoulder.

"We should go some time. Maybe not with him," he replies, nodding behind him. "Too competitive."

"He is, isn't he?" It feels nice to be able to talk about Nate with someone who knows him. And who will gossip. "Was he always like that?"

"Oh man, always. We're like, ten years old, playing lacrosse on our school team, and coach was constantly having to pull him back during practice 'cause he was always going full out, full contact."

He and I laugh together. I notice Nate pause in his stroke, but I can't imagine he can hear us.

"Do you still play lacrosse?"

"Naw, I don't really have the discipline to keep up with it. I was good in high school, but you have to be great to cut it in college. What sport do you play?"

"Oh, none."

"Really? You look like you're so in shape."

"Oh, thanks," I reply, managing to only blush a bit. From anyone else it would have seemed like a ham-fisted compliment, but Jackson has such a natural, easygoing way about him.

"You going to this party in Georgetown tonight?" he asks, dunking his head briefly underneath the water, then shaking off his hair like a dog.

"What party?"

"Oh, I figured Nate told you."

"Told her what?" Nate asks, appearing next to him.

"'Bout Chris's party," Jackson replies nonchalantly. Nate's jaw muscles twitch.

"Hadn't mentioned it," he replies shortly.

"Well, you should come," Jackson says, turning back to me.

"She's not going to know anyone, and I think it's just gonna be a small thing," Nate says.

"Dude, Chris said to invite anyone. They've got the whole townhouse. It's gonna be great."

"I just—" Nate begins, as I bite my lip. Here I thought we were maybe getting along better, despite the awkwardness, and now he's going out of his way to exclude me.

"If you're worried about being a third wheel, just invite Dana or someone," Jackson says, though even when he's arguing, he doesn't seem to have a care in the world. "So, what do you think?" he asks me.

"Sounds great, actually," I say, glancing at Nate, feeling a bit gratified as he glares at me. It feels good to spite him a little, since he so clearly doesn't want me to go.

"Awesome. Tonight then. We can go together— I'll pick you guys up around ten," Jackson says, before jumping on top of Nate and trying to wrestle him under the water.

I close my eyes as they disappear. For the first time in a while, I wish I had something cute to wear.

CHAPTER TEN

* * *

In the end, I have to go with the same black top I wore to that crew party. It's really my only top suitable for a party, I think. Besides, Nate's the only one who's seen me in it, and I doubt he remembers.

My mom excitedly waves goodbye as Nate and I walk out to Jackson's green SUV. She is so thrilled that I might have a social life that it's embarrassing. Jackson opens up the front passenger door for me and Nate slides in back.

"We picking up Dana?" Jackson asks as we pull away.

"It's Natasha tonight. And she's meeting us there," Nate answers from the back seat. I guess I'm relieved, because I don't think I could look Dana in the eye after seeing her and Nate having sex by the pool.

"Oh, fuck, Natasha, of course," Jackson says, laughing and hitting the steering wheel. I frown a little. I guess it's par for the course for my stepbrother.

Jackson picks up most of the slack in the conversation, and the radio does the rest. I'm too nervous and stuck in my head, thinking of what I should say, while Nate mumbles one word responses from the back.

I'm relieved when we find a parking space on the street near the party. As we walk toward the riotous townhouse, I'm surprised the neighbors haven't already called the cops. People are spilling out the front door and I can hear the music halfway down the block. There's a pretty olive-skinned girl standing on the curb who turns her head as Nate calls out, "Natasha!"

She smiles coyly as we walk up. Nate dips her in a jokingly romantic manner and plants a kiss on her lips as she breaks out into giggles.

"Come on," Jackson says, draping an arm around my shoulders protectively and escorting me inside.

He high-fives a few guys as we walk in, and he guides me to a keg in the middle of the living room, which is strung with little white Christmas lights. There's an impenetrable crowd around it but somehow he manages to snag me a beer, and before I know it I'm taking my first sip of the summer. With his hand on the small of my back, we walk into the next room. The dining room table is being used for a beer pong game, and Jackson and I take a seat on a couch nearby.

"You're gorgeous, you know that?" Jackson whispers in my ear. I'm startled and almost spit out my beer.

"No…" I look down, blushing, "I mean, that's sweet of you to say."

"I'd love to see you again after tonight. Maybe we could get dinner next weekend," he offers.

"Oh, sure," I reply, feeling flattered. I mean, it does feel a little…rushed, or something, but I've heard so many stories about guys just wanting to hook up, that it's refreshing to be asked out on an old-fashioned date. I take a few more sips of my beer as I look around, feeling more comfortable now that I know Jackson is really into me.

"Hey, I'm going to get another beer," I tell Jackson, as I drain mine. He jumps up.

"Don't worry about it. I'll grab 'em," he says, walking confidently into the other room. I watch the ping pong ball as it's thrown back and forth across the table, and Jackson is soon back with the beers. He launches into a story about this crazy party he went to back at school, but out of the corner of my eye I notice a couple walking up the stairs at the rear of the room, their hands all over each other, and feel a stab of envy in my chest.

I am beyond tired of being a virgin. It's certainly not on purpose that I'm twenty-one and still haven't had sex yet. I guess I just assumed it would happen somehow, without my ever putting any thought into it, and I've never built it up like it's going to be some crazy special thing, either.

I look at Jackson out of the corner of my eye as I make quick work of my second beer. Maybe Nate was right—maybe I am too serious and distant.

Maybe it would be better if I just got it out of the way. And I bet Jackson would be good at it. Really, really good at it. Plus, he's a decent guy.

"…Don't you think?" Jackson asks me, leaning in.

"Yes, right," I reply, even though I spaced out and have no idea what he was talking about. My hair falls in front of my face as I take another sip of beer, and Jackson reaches up and tucks it behind my ear. We make eye contact and he leans forward slowly, brushing a soft kiss across my neck.

"Want to get out of here?" he murmurs into my ear, sending a little shiver down my spine. "My place is pretty close by, and we'll actually be able to hear ourselves think."

"Um, yeah, that sounds good," I reply, a little nervously. Jackson stands and offers me his hand. I place mine in his and he leads me out toward the front. We pass Nate on the way, with his arms wrapped around Natasha and his hands tucked into her back pockets.

"Hey man, we're taking off. You think you can find another ride?" Jackson asks.

"What do you mean? You're both leaving?" Nate asks, frowning.

"Yup, we're going back to my place, dude," Jackson replies. "You cool for a ride?"

"Yeah, come here for a second," Nate says, his eyes flicking back and forth between us. He takes Jackson's arm and pulls him toward a screen door in the back. "Not you," he says to me, as I begin to follow.

I bristle at his tone. They disappear out back and I look after them, my mouth open in shock and annoyance. I can't believe the way Nate talks to me sometimes. So dismissively. I exchange a polite smile with Natasha, who is now looking around the party aimlessly, clearly bored without Nate.

Screw Nate. I'll do whatever the hell I please, and I want to know what he's saying.

I brush past Natasha, push open the screen door and walk into the small, fenced-in backyard. There are fewer people out here, but there's still a crowd. I can just see Nate and Jackson talking in a back corner. I weave my way through the people, keeping my head down so they don't notice me. I take out my phone so I look like I'm doing something other than eavesdropping, and sidle into the group nearest to them. I can just overhear what they're saying.

"Why, do *you* want her Nate?" Jackson asks angrily. My eyes widen.

"Fuck no, she's my stepsister. It's just weird, that's all. You two. She's not your type." I feel a stab of pain at the finality of Nate's words.

"She's gorgeous," I hear Jackson reply.

"You think she's gorgeous?" Nate says, beginning to laugh. "Seriously? Dude, come on. Besides, she's a fucking buzz kill."

I don't want to hear any more. I can already feel angry tears building up behind my eyes. I'm so stupid. Why do I keep giving Nate the benefit of the doubt, when he is so clearly such an asshole?

I walk quickly back inside, through the living room, and out to the street. I turn toward the left, where I can see a busier street, and hustle toward it. I know it's going to be a pricey cab ride back to the house, but I feel like I'm about to explode into a puddle of tears.

And I don't want to give Nate the satisfaction of seeing me cry.

CHAPTER ELEVEN

* * *

I breathe in as deeply as possible and hold it, counting to ten before exhaling as slowly as I can, trying to rid myself of the hurt feeling that followed me home from the party. It's a trick I learned to control my anxiety, and to say that I'm anxious right now would be an understatement.

I can't remember the last time I heard someone talk about me like that, though I suppose it's partially my fault for eavesdropping. I finally start to feel calm enough to go to sleep, and reach to turn off my bedside lamp.

A rush of footsteps up the stairs makes me pause. I sit up a bit as they continue down the hallway toward my bedroom. A second later, my bedroom door bursts open and Nate walks in, his face dark with anger.

"You're in bed? You've gotta be fucking kidding me. That was really selfish of you to run off without telling anyone, you know that?" he spits at me, then turns around and walks out.

I'm frozen in shock for a moment. What the hell was that? What does he have to be mad at me for? I leap out from under my covers and march out of my bedroom just in time to stop him from shutting his door. He swings around as I charge into his room.

"*I'm* selfish? You are just…you are just…" I stumble in my anger, trying to think of the right word.

"Yeah, you're selfish, Brynn! I looked around that party for you for thirty minutes! I thought you might have been kidnapped! I almost called the cops!"

"Wait…what?" I reply, completely thrown.

"Ever heard of a text message?" he asks, his voice laden with sarcasm.

"Yes, I've heard of a text message!" Man, I wish I were better at arguing. "Hey, wait a second, this isn't about me, this is about you! You're the asshole! I heard what you were saying about me to Jackson, I'm not a buzzkill, and maybe I'm not gorgeous, but I'm not some kind of joke, either!" I fight back the tears welling in my eyes, more angry than I've ever been in my life. There, that got him. He stands dumbfounded and I seize the opportunity to walk out.

Just as I'm about to cross the threshold, he reaches around me and closes the door in front of me. I stop short and turn around angrily, almost ready to smack him. He's standing so close to me I'm practically pinned against the door.

"Wait, what? How'd you hear that? You followed us outside?"

"Yes, I followed you," I reply, stumbling a bit because I know I was wrong in that regard. "I was mad because you were obviously trying to stop me from leaving with Jackson, and I wanted to know why." I take a deep breath. "I guess I can't control what you think about me, and that's…whatever, that's fine, but I don't know why you had to go sharing your opinion with Jackson. I mean, am I really that unattractive to you?"

To my horror, my lower lip starts to tremble. I don't want to cry right now but I can't hold back the tears any longer.

"No…shit, that's not what…" Nate says, his eyes widen as a tear slips down my cheek. I furiously brush it away and Nate backs up, running his hands through his wavy hair. "It's not that I don't want Jackson to date you, it's that I don't want you to date Jackson."

"What? That doesn't make any sense," I reply, trying to staunch the flow of tears as I tug at my hair.

"Jackson's track record with women is pretty bad. They're just conquests to him."

I cross my arms and frown at him. "That sounds pretty hypocritical. I mean, the first time we met, you asked me to have a threesome with you and you didn't even know my name."

A smile tugs at the corner of his mouth. "OK, that's fair. For the record, you just looked so shocked, and innocent—I couldn't resist. You're right, it's not like I have a great track record either. I guess the difference, in my mind, is that I'm upfront about it.

I've never promised a woman a relationship. The girls I sleep with, they know that it's not going anywhere because I tell them that. Jackson pulls them in by promising them a future with him, and then as soon as he sleeps with them, he acts like they don't exist."

"But you're friends with him…" I point out.

"Well, he's a good friend. Loyal, funny…"

"But he sounds like a bad person. I just… I don't know why you'd want to be friends with a person like that. Sorry, maybe I'm just…" I shake my head, trying to process this new version of events. "He did…what you just said about him does match up with some things he was saying to me. God, I can't believe I fell for it."

"He wasn't always like that," Nate says quietly, gesturing vaguely to a framed photo sitting on his desk. I glance at it, then walk over to get a closer look.

"Oh my god, is that you?" I ask, picking it up. It's a class photo from elementary school, three rows of smiling kids with their teacher standing next to them.

Nate is easy to spot. "You look so serious, like you're on the way to the office or something."

Nate peers over my shoulder at it, his face an exact reflection of his younger self. "That was the year my mom left," he says quietly.

"Oh. Oh, I'm sorry. Do you ever see her?"

"No. She made her choice." He pauses for a moment. "That one's Jackson," he says, pointing out a grinning towheaded boy. I snort. He had a flirtatious smile even back then. "I'm sorry you heard me say those things. Jackson's the kind of guy who, if you tell him something's off limits, that makes him want it even more. He's never been denied anything. So I thought it would be better to convince him that he didn't want you in the first place."

I fiddle with the edge of the frame and then turn to face him. He's standing closer than I thought he was. "So…you don't think those things about me?" I whisper, feeling suddenly vulnerable.

"No, the exact opposite, really," he replies, equally softly. "Brynn you are gorgeous."

There's a charged moment between us. I can't rip my gaze away from his eyes. I realize he's moving forward ever so slowly, and my lips automatically part, my body taking over from my brain. Every inch of my skin tingles, and I suddenly feel brave—a completely different reaction than anything I've ever felt being this close to Jackson.

Just before his mouth touches mine, I close my eyes. As our lips come together, an exquisite feeling rushes through me, unlike anything I've ever felt before. His lips graze mine, then return a bit more firmly, guiding me into a kiss. I've been kissed by a handful of guys over the years, but this kiss is something else. Nate is something else.

His hands wrap around my waist and slide to the small of my back as his lips crush against mine. All my thoughts evaporate, all my worries and insecurities—maybe it's that I can tell he knows exactly what he's doing, and so I can let myself go, trust myself in his hands. He nudges me slightly with his nose and his lower lip brushes against mine. I almost gasp as I feel his tongue move smoothly into my mouth. Electricity flies straight from my mouth to the base of my hips.

I press my tongue against his as my hands move of their own accord up to his chest. I lay my palms against his pecs and feel his racing heartbeat under his rapidly rising and falling chest. It's my first hint that there's something else hiding under his completely confident exterior.

His tongue moves deeper into my mouth, and his hands pull me close against his body. I wrap my arms around his neck and run my fingers through the hair falling onto the collar of his polo. I can feel his erection pushing against my stomach as he slides one hand over my ass. I want nothing more than to rip my clothes off, jump on his bed, and be ravaged by him…to feel his mouth all over my body…inside me…

Suddenly he pulls away. I almost fall forward in surprise as my eyes blink open.

"I shouldn't have done that," he mutters.

"Why?" I whisper, falling quickly from my cloud.

"It's wrong…you're my stepsister. Maybe it's best if we just keep our distance from each other."

"Yeah, you're right…" I reply, feeling like he's just slapped me in the face. I walk quickly to the door. I pause before I open it, wishing I could put into words what I'm feeling, but I can't. I open the door and close it softly behind me before rushing to my room.

As I curl up under the covers, I try to wrap my mind around all the twists this night has taken. I can't believe Nate and I just kissed. I mean, I've been dreaming about that moment since I first laid eyes on him freshman year. I've found that most things in life don't live up to how I've built them up in my head, but that kiss far surpassed any fantasy. I can feel my body reacting at just the thought of his lips touching mine again.

But is he right? Was it wrong of us to do that? Light is creeping around the sides of my shades by the time I manage to fall asleep, and I still haven't managed to find an answer.

CHAPTER TWELVE

* * *

Nate and I pass the next few weeks as though we're each surrounded by an invisible force field. Whenever one of us enters a room, the other is propelled out of it. We're only pushed into close proximity with each other when we have a family dinner, though my mom has been pushing those on us quite frequently in an effort to bond.

If she only knew.

Today, though, Nate's and my presence is required at the same event: the Thornhill's annual Fourth of July party. It's in our very own backyard, starting in the afternoon with a crab boil and extending through the evening fireworks. Apparently we'll get a good view of the country club's annual fireworks display just down the river.

My mom has absolutely insisted on buying me a new dress for the occasion, and even came into the fitting room with me to make sure it fit correctly. The shift dress is not exactly my style, but I've seen it on plenty of girls at school. I'm just worried about spilling tartar sauce on the bright white fabric. I pull on my new pair of gold wedges, and walk downstairs to see if my mom needs any help.

I'm taken aback by the flurry of activity downstairs. As I walk outside, I realize I've underestimated the scale of this party. When I heard "crab boil," I was picturing a few picnic tables with red and white tablecloths, but this is clearly a classy affair. There are elegant round tables set, with flowing linens and extravagant centerpieces on top of them. The food is presented in silver trays, and garlands festoon the perimeter. I spot my mom talking in hushed, urgent tones to one of the caterers, and head over.

"Oh, Brynn, you look beautiful! That dress fits you so well," she gushes.

"Thanks…do you need any help?"

"Mmm, no. I think we're OK. The guests should begin arriving in about ten minutes. Oh, go taste the

Freedom Martini over at the bar and tell me what you think. I'm worried it's a little too sweet."

"The Freedom Martini?"

"The signature cocktail we created for this event," the caterer next to her chimes in with a chipper grin.

"Ah, of course," I reply, heading for the bar. The bartender serves me a pale pink drink and I take a sip. Not too sweet—it's delicious, light and refreshing. Luckily the day isn't too hot, anyway. The temperature has managed to stay below ninety degrees for the party.

I decide to go down to the river since I'd just feel in the way while they're setting up. I walk down to the lower lawn and down the steps. As I reach the shore, I navigate the rocky sand cautiously in my heels. A splash on the other side of the large boulder grabs my attention. I walk toward it and peer around. Nate's standing there, skipping rocks with a smooth sidearm motion. I pause, admiring his form, then decide it's best to just go back up to the lawn before he notices me. He's made it clear he doesn't want to talk to me.

I turn back and as I walk my heel catches on a rock. I gasp as I slip sideways, and feel two strong hands catching me under my arms to hold me up.

"Whoa, careful," he says as he straightens me up.

"Thanks," I reply as I turn to him and tuck my hair back behind my ears. "You escaping from the commotion, too?"

"Yeah. I don't really enjoy these things."

"Really? You're so…" I trail off.

"What?" he asks with a grin.

I groan. "Fine. I was going to say 'charming,' OK?"

"I knew it," he replies jokingly. "Well, whatever charm you might be noticing has been developed over many years of practice. My dad has been dragging me to these kinds of events for years. I know the routine. Smile, shake hands, tell the kinds of jokes that don't make anyone think too hard."

"Sounds…horrible. But at least there's a lot of free food." He gives me a bemused glance. "Right.

Sometimes I forget I don't have to worry about that stuff anymore."

"You were, um, not well-off before our parents—" he drops his gaze.

"I'd say we were struggling. But it was just the way I grew up. I never wanted for anything big, though we certainly frequented the Goodwill racks often enough. But I don't want you to think…I mean, my mom, she really cares for Pierce."

"Relax—I don't think your mom's a gold digger. There have always been some of those around, and I can practically smell them at this point. I mean, maybe at first I was worried, but I'm not now."

"Was your mom—" I begin, feeling brave.

"I don't like to talk about her," he cuts me off, and chucks another rock out onto the water. It hits the surface with a plopping sound and sinks.

"Sorry," I whisper. "How's your shoulder?"

"Hurts," he replies shortly.

"I'll see you up there," I say after a moment, since he's clearly done with the conversation.

"Hey," he calls after me as I climb the steps. "Jackson and his parents are here. They're family friends. They're on the guest list every year."

"Got it, thanks," I reply, before mounting the rest of the steps. That was considerate of him, and it sounds like he was telling me that he didn't invite Jackson himself.

As I walk across the lawn, I can see that the first guests are beginning to arrive. I wonder if now that I'm Pierce's stepdaughter, I'm going be expected to put on the same song-and-dance routine as Nate. Usually if I have to go to a party, like my aunt's Christmas party, I'll hang out for a while, and then disappear somewhere to read a book.

My fears are realized as my mom waves me over to where she and Pierce are standing with two guests. I'm introduced to the couple, who turn out to be higher-ups for the State Department, and my accomplishments are trotted out while they murmur enthusiastically, though I have to wonder if anyone could possibly be genuinely interested in such self-serving prattle. As we talk, my mom breaks away to greet the guests that are now pouring in. I listen politely as Pierce chats away, impressed with his wit and charm. Clearly Nate gets it from his dad, even if he does insist that it's a learned skill.

I manage to slip away and head over to the buffet table. Like any good Maryland girl, I absolutely love crabs. As I pile my plate high, I feel a hand on the small of my back. I turn to see Jackson grinning at me. With his open, friendly face, it's hard to keep in mind what Nate told me about him, and what I experienced for myself.

"Hey, Brynn!" he says, brushing a kiss against my cheek.

"Jackson, good to see you," I reply politely.

"You disappeared so fast the last time I saw you! I was worried," he replies.

"Sorry about that," I respond, wondering if Nate gave him any explanation.

"We ever going to go on that date?"

I'm saved by the sight of Allison walking out onto the deck. "Could you excuse me for a moment? My best friend just got here and she doesn't know anyone else," I explain as I slip away. I wave at her as I approach, but she's looking around nervously and doesn't register my presence.

"Allison!" I call out, just ten feet from her.

"Oh! Oh my gosh, I didn't recognize you," she says. I give her a hug as I walk up. "This party is really fancy! And this house! I mean you said it was big, but I didn't think it was *this* big."

"I know," I groan. "I'll give you a tour later if you have a couple hours," I add wryly. "Come get something to eat with me—I was just filling up a plate. I'm so glad you're here. I don't really know anyone else, and none of the interns have shown up yet."

"The interns?" Allison asks as we head back over to the buffet, where I pick up my abandoned plate.

"Yeah, Pierce invited all the interns from the office."

"Oh, that was nice of him," Allison comments, picking up her own plate. "Wow, I think that guy's a senator…the one in the blue seersucker jacket."

I glance over. "From Georgia, yeah," I confirm. "I think he and Pierce served in Congress at the same time." I start giggling and Allison looks at me with a questioning smile. "Sorry, I just can't believe I'm talking about *my* stepfather serving in congress."

"This is your real life!" Allison says, laughing. "When do you think it'll sink in?"

"No idea," I reply as we head toward a couple empty seats at one of the tables.

"Your mom looks really happy," Allison observes as we sit. I watch her for a moment, flitting between conversations, so beautiful and animated.

"I think she is. And she's just really good at cocktail-type conversation, too. Like Nate, though he says it doesn't come to him naturally."

"Brynn…" Allison says, raising an eyebrow at me.

"No, I mean, I'm just, you know…" I reply, trailing off. Definitely not the time to tell Allison that Nate and I kissed, though I don't know if that time will ever come. I love Allison, but thinking in shades of grey is not her strong suit.

"Thought you two could use some drinks."

I look up to see Greg, the cute intern with the strawberry-blonde hair, standing next to us, three martini glasses carefully balanced between his long fingers.

"Greg, hi! I'm so glad you could make it." I indicate the chair next to us and help him place down the glasses so that they don't spill their contents. "Greg, this is my friend Allison. We go to college together."

"Nice to meet you," Allison says.

"You too. Hope these drinks are OK with you. I forget what the bartender called them…"

"Freedom Martinis," I answer, rolling my eyes. "The name sucks, but they're really good."

"So where are you from originally, Greg?" Allison asks.

"Raleigh, though I hope to move to DC after I graduate."

I tune out slightly as Allison and Greg talk across me. I've just seen Nate cross between groups of people, seeming to make conversation effortlessly. I look around to see if there's a girl trailing him, but I don't see one. This might be the first time I've seen him without a date at any kind of gathering. The idea that it could be because of me comes to my mind, but I quickly quash it. I can't let myself think like that. Nate doesn't want that kind of relationship with me, probably even if I weren't his stepsister. I bet his date just got a cold last-minute or something.

"Be right back," Allison says. "I have to get a second helping!"

My attention snaps back to Greg as she stands and leaves. He scratches his cheek and clears his throat. I smile as a blush sneaks onto his freckle-dotted skin.

"You look…um, that's a nice dress," he finally says.

"Thanks." I smile, careful not to linger on the subject, "So, you think you'll want to work in politics after school ends?"

"Well, in government," he says with a smile. "Though I'm learning that one doesn't seem to exist without the other. I guess I need to work on the whole…you know…" he waves his hand vaguely.

"Kissing babies thing?"

"Exactly," he smiles. "So, ah, I was wondering…"

My attention drifts from him again as I see my mom and Pierce talking urgently by the house. My mom covers her face with her hands and Pierce turns back to the party, his frown turning into a smile as if by magic.

"I'm so sorry, Greg, could you excuse me? I think my mom might need me."

"Oh, sure," he replies kindly as I rush toward the door into the study.

My mind runs through the possible scenarios as I hurry through the study and up the stairs. As I climb the second set of stairs up to the master suite on the third floor, I decide it must be my father. The last time I saw my mom look that upset, it was because my dad was back in town and pressuring her for money.

I knock softly on the closed double door of their bedroom. "Mom?" I whisper quietly as I let myself in. "What's wrong?" I gasp as I hurry in. She's curled up on top of the bedspread, like a broken doll.

"It's Pierce," she murmurs without moving. "His lawyer just called him. A woman has come forward accusing him of sexual harassment. It'll be on the news tomorrow."

CHAPTER THIRTEEN

* * *

"Oh no," I whisper, sitting next to her on the bed. "I'm so sorry, Mom."

"Is it…is it me?" she asks, turning her head as a tear drops down her cheek.

"What? What do you mean?"

"Maybe it's me…maybe it's my fault. It's like I'm a curse."

"No, Mom, no," I whisper, leaning down and pulling her hair out of her eyes. "This isn't happening because of you. I mean, when did this even go on? The, you know, the…" I reply, unable to repeat those two ugly words: sexual harassment.

"Several years ago," she replies.

"Long before he ever met you," I point out. "So, what? This woman's going on TV?"

My mom nods. "One of those investigation shows is doing a piece about sexual harassment in politics, and she's going to be interviewed."

"What are you going to do?"

"Well, we'll have to batten down the hatches. We'll probably have to stay in the house for a few days, though luckily tomorrow's Saturday anyway."

"No, that's not what I meant. I mean, if Pierce sexually harassed a—"

"I don't want to think about it."

"Mom, you have to," I sigh. She's always been like the child in our relationship. I'm tired of the dynamic, but I don't know how to break the pattern without our entire relationship falling apart. "If Pierce did that, then maybe you have to—"

"Don't say it. Pierce and I are staying together. That's not a question. And even if he did do it, I'm sure it was a momentary weakness. It was just something that happened a long time ago, and he's changed."

I shrug, feeling helpless. "I want that to be true, Mom, I really do. Not for his sake, but for yours. I did hear a rumor at work, though," I say hesitatingly.

"What do you mean? What kind of rumor?"

"That…Pierce has a certain reputation."

"Why didn't you tell me?"

I want to tell her that it's because she's so fragile, but instead I just reply, "Because it was just a rumor that I heard from one person. I had no way of knowing if it were true."

"Well, until there's some evidence or something, I'm going to believe Pierce. He said she was a woman at work who was denied a promotion she wanted, and now she's starting a jewelry line, and thought she might as well put her bitterness to good use and drum up some publicity."

"I guess that could be it," I say without conviction.

My mom nods. "I think I just want to be alone for a while. Do you think you could go back to the party, and sort of act like the hostess for me? You know, make sure everyone's having a good time and all that? Just say I have a headache if anyone asks after me."

"Um, alright," I reply, not knowing what else to say.

"Thanks, honey," my mom says, settling back onto the pillow. I stand and head for the door. "I just can't believe it," I hear her murmur as I close the bedroom door behind me. I wish I didn't believe it either, but there's a telltale knot in the pit of my stomach that's telling me I do.

I head back down to the party, taking the stairs slowly. I'd rather be doing pretty much anything else right now than plastering a smile on my face and pretending everything's fine. But I know my mom's right—it will look odd if both of us disappear during the party. I reemerge out back and take a deep breath as I cross back over to Greg and Allison.

"Sorry about that. My mom has a headache, I just wanted to check on her," I relay dutifully. Greg and Allison murmur sympathetically. I finish the rest of my food quickly, and with only one ear on their conversation, before standing up with my drink. I excuse myself and begin to mingle, trying to circulate and play the part of the hostess like my mom asked.

I watch the fading light impatiently; willing the sun to set as fast as possible so that this party can finally be over. The chipper event organizer I met earlier appears quietly at my side as I force a laugh at a partygoer's joke.

"Have you seen Mrs. Thornhill?"

It still throws me to hear my mom referred to like that. "She's not feeling well. Can I help you with something?"

"Would you like the lanterns to be lit now, or should we wait?"

I glance around at the dimming light. "Now would be fine, thanks." She hurries away and I spot Nate across the party, frowning at me. I avert my gaze quickly. If his dad hasn't told him what's going on yet, I don't want the task to fall on me. I see him making his way over, and excuse myself from my current conversation to disappear into a large group of people around the pool. Just another hour or so and the fireworks will be done, and everyone will leave.

The caterers move throughout the party, lighting candles on the tables and mini Chinese lanterns strung in the trees. I take a moment to admire the scene: the beautiful white lights, the well-heeled crowd, the murmur of easy conversation. My mom does know how to throw a good party. I grab another drink as the twilight turns into night and people begin heading down to the lower lawn to get a better view of the fireworks.

With a sudden *boom*, the display begins. There are a few exclamations of excitement and some clapping as the crowd gathers to stare downriver at the explosions of color. I'm making my way toward the rear of the crowd when I feel a hand on the small of my back. I know before I even turn around that it's Nate.

"What's going on?" he asks quietly, as I turn to face him.

"It's nothing. My mom just isn't feeling well," I reply.

"You're pulling at your hair," he points out, and I drop my hand, feeling caught. The crowd cheers as an especially colorful firework goes off above us.

"So?"

"I can read you like a book, Brynn," he replies, leaning in. I can feel his breath on my cheek and step back, feeling flustered.

"I just think it's something that your dad should tell you," I say, and turn back to the fireworks, but I feel his hand on my elbow.

"Would you just tell me? You and my dad are both acting strangely, and now your mom disappears…I just want to know."

"And here I thought I was covering well," I say, stalling for time.

"Maybe to other people, but not to me." I stare at him for a moment as his features are illuminated by the light of one of my favorite, willow-shaped fireworks.

"There's a woman…she's going to go on the news tomorrow and say that your dad sexually harassed her."

"That's crazy," he hisses at me.

"I'm just the messenger—you insisted I tell you—" I stammer, taken aback by his tone.

"My dad, he's a great man. He's a pillar of the community—"

"A pillar of the community?"

"What? He is!"

"It's just, sometimes the way you talk about him…he's not perfect, Nate."

"You don't know anything about him. When my mom abandoned us, he took care of me all by himself. He's always been there for me."

"OK, I'm just—"

But Nate storms off back to the house. I stand in shock for a moment. I knew that conversation wasn't going to be fun, but I didn't think he'd turn on me like that, as though I were attacking Pierce, or something.

I turn back toward the crowd just as the finale begins and the sky lights up. I glance at the people around me, their faces upturned, their expressions joyous. Maybe it was silly of me to look forward to everyone leaving. Because now I realize that tomorrow, it will be back to the four of us alone in the house—and no buffer zone.

My eyes fall on Pierce and I realize he's staring at me. He smiles quickly when he realizes that I'm looking at him, and leads the applause as the last firework dies out.

CHAPTER FOURTEEN

* * *

I was half-worried that the plan was for all four of us to watch the TV program together, but thankfully there's no such expectation. Or at least, I haven't been told of it. It's the first time in a while my mom hasn't insisted on a family dinner. She's been holed up in her room most of the day, while Pierce fields calls from his attorneys in his study.

I decide to grab some leftover pasta from the fridge to eat in my room, and peer into Nate's room as I pass. No sign of him.

I shut my door behind me and open my computer to check out some of the coverage online. I feel nauseous as I read the woman's claims, though slightly relieved that she isn't accusing Pierce of any kind of violence. She talks mostly about lingering touches, shoulder massages, and being stonewalled by management when she complained.

I finish eating and click around the internet for a while, feeling restless. When I can't stand my boredom any longer, I take my plate and walk back down to the kitchen and put it in the dishwasher. The phone on the counter rings as I'm headed past it. I pause for a moment, waiting to see if someone else is going to answer it. What if it's a reporter? Do I just say 'no comment,' like they do on TV?

On the third ring, I decide to bite the bullet. "Hello?"

"Hi, is Nate there?" a female voice asks breathlessly. Ah, another admirer.

"Sorry, I don't think he is," I reply honestly. "Can I take a message?"

There's a slight pause. "Is this Holly?"

"No, this is her daughter, Brynn. May I ask who's calling?" There's another long pause, and I begin to feel uneasy.

"It's Eileen…Nate's mom."

I almost drop the phone in surprise. "Oh, um, I don't—"

"Wait! Please, please don't hang up. I just saw the news, and thought that Nate might be willing to talk to me now."

"I don't understand."

"Because he'll know the truth about Pierce, and then maybe he won't believe whatever he says about me."

"I'm sorry, I don't think I should be in the middle of this." Whatever it is.

"Please, please…" I hear her gasp and the clear sound of crying. "I haven't talked to Nate in so long…he's my son, he's my son."

"But you chose to leave him…"

"Is that what Pierce told you?"

"No, Nate."

"He heard it from Pierce. I left Pierce because he was *cheating* on me. But Pierce is used to having everything his own way, and he was furious. He was the one with the money, I came into the marriage with nothing, and signed a pre-nup. I mean, I barely even looked at the thing at the time—I thought we'd be together forever. He had an expensive lawyer and managed to get full custody in the divorce. I never had a chance. I've been trying to get in touch with Nate for years to tell him the truth…I left Pierce, not Nate. I would never leave my son. I never would have divorced Pierce, even though he was cheating on me, if I had known I'd never see my son again. I thought after seeing this woman on TV, maybe he'd believe me…" She dissolves into sobs.

"Eileen, Eileen, it's OK," I whisper, feeling sick. Something about what she's telling me rings true. I can feel it in my gut. "I want to help you, but…Nate, he's really touchy about his father. I don't know what I can do."

"I know, and I'm sorry to put this on you. I call the house now and then trying to get Nate, and I was just hoping that he would pick up tonight and not hang up on me."

A sound behind me makes me fly around. Pierce is standing in the doorway to the dining room.

"Everything OK?" he asks.

"Yep, everything's fine, Pierce," I reply so that Eileen can hear me.

"Just take down my number, alright?" Eileen says quietly. "Please, just tell him what I said." I write the number down on a small notepad on the counter, conscious that Pierce is watching me.

"Got it, thanks. Talk to you later," I say, and hang up.

"Not a reporter, I hope," Pierce says with a sad smile.

"No, just a friend," I reply as nonchalantly as possible, and rip the paper off the pad and stuff it in my pocket.

"God, this has been the longest day of my life," he says with a sigh, running his fingers through his hair. "I hope you and your mom don't get dragged into anything. There might be some reporters hanging out by the gate tomorrow. Probably best to just avoid them."

"Sure, no problem." He looks so tired, and I find myself quickly feeling sorry for him. He seems so genuine right now that it's hard to believe what Eileen and this other woman are saying about him. The man in front of me paints such a different picture.

"On the other hand, though, I'm glad that you and your mom are here right now. Maybe it's selfish of me. But I don't think I'd make it through all this without her. She's really brought light back into my life."

"She's…yeah, she's great," I reply awkwardly.

"Are you having a good time at the internship? Not too much busy work, I hope."

"No, not at all, Pierce. It's wonderful, thank you."

He nods. "Well, I better get back to work. You'd think I'd have gotten a lot done, considering how long I've been in there, but I've just been staring at the wall."

"Oh, well, I'll see you tomorrow then."

"'Night."

"Goodnight." I walk back upstairs with the phone number burning a hole in my pocket. It's amazing to me that I've gone from being almost sure that Pierce is lying, to feeling like I've betrayed his trust in the span of one short conversation with him. Is he telling the truth, or does he just possess a consummate politician's ability to spin the story for himself?

I get ready for bed slowly, my mind wandering uncontrollably. Before this summer, I felt sure of things in my life. Sure of my ideas and opinions. Sure that I was right. But I feel less and less sure of myself the longer I stay in this house.

Just as I finish brushing my teeth, I hear a thud from the hallway, then a groan. That sounded like Nate. With a frown, I open my bedroom door. Sure enough, there's Nate, lying on the carpet just outside his own room. I hesitate, realizing I'm wearing my little nightgown, but figure he's seen me in it already.

"Nate? Are you OK? What happened?" I murmur, hurrying to kneel next to him. The whiff of alcohol coming off of him gives it away before he says anything.

"I'm so drunk, Brynn," he says, beginning to laugh.

"Shhh, you'll wake up our parents," I admonish him. "Why are you on the floor?"

"Tripped. On my own foot," he replies with a sigh.

"Well, come on, get up," I order him, sliding a hand under his torso to pull him upward. He slowly obeys and stands on his feet, where he sways dangerously. "OK, now in here," I continue, pushing his bedroom door open with my foot as I slide an arm around his back to stabilize him. I feel his muscles clench under his t-shirt as we walk. *Not the time, Brynn.* "Shoes off," I order him as we reach the bed.

"Mmm," he grunts, as he kicks them off.

"I'm getting you some water. Don't move." I hurry back to my bedroom and grab my water glass from the bedside table, then refill it from the tap in my bathroom before heading back to his room. I shut the door behind me to keep the noise from filtering around the house, then stop in surprise as I see that Nate has stripped down to his boxers and is standing at the foot of his bed.

"Thanks," he slurs, as I hesitantly walk forward and hand him the water. I watch him gulp the whole glass down, the grey moonlight from the window illuminating his ripped torso. He puts the glass down on his desk and wipes his mouth with the back of his hand as he sways slightly.

"You alright?" I ask worriedly. "I've never seen you drunk before."

"Don't really drink. No time. Work, practice, work, game."

"And I thought I was the nerd," I tease him.

"You're funny," he says, cocking his head slightly, then takes a step toward me.

"Nate…" I say as my core clenches.

"Yes, Brynn?" he asks innocently.

"You said this was wrong. Those were your words," I remind him.

"Do *you* think it's wrong?" He takes another step toward me, and looks down at me.

"I—"

His hand reaches around my waist. "Does it *feel* wrong?"

"Yes…No," I breathe. I barely have time to inhale before his mouth is on mine. His mouth tastes like whiskey, but I don't care. I wrap my hands around his neck and he grabs my ass with both hands, our kiss picking up right where our last one broke off. I dig my fingers into his hair as our mouths open to one another. He pulls me roughly against him and groans deep in his throat as our bodies collide. Suddenly he stumbles back, steadying himself on my shoulders.

"Sorry," he whispers, shaking his head as though to clear it. "Will you just stay with me for a while?"

"Yes, of course," I reply immediately, even though I'm taken aback by his request. I watch him turn to his bed and crawl over to his pillow, then curl up on his side and look at me expectantly. I pause, then follow him, crawling across the bedspread and curling around his back. I bury my head between his shoulder blades then drape my arm over his waist, and feel him take my hand in his and pull me closer against him.

I lie as still as I can, barely breathing. I can't believe he's letting me touch him like this. Well, he is wasted, but still. I never thought he'd be so vulnerable around me. I hear his breathing deepen.

"I've always looked up to him," he murmurs, startling me.

"I know," I whisper back, knowing that he's talking about his dad.

"I don't know what I would do if he—"

"I know," I murmur, softly kissing the back of his neck. He stills on his pillow, and his breathing slows down again.

I stay with him for a while, until I know he's asleep. I need to understand Nate's feelings about his mother before I tell him what she told me. His world is already falling apart around him, and I don't want to make it happen faster. I sigh. I should probably go back to my room.

* * *

I turn over with a sigh and frown. My sheets feel different, and the light coming in from the window is much too bright. I blink my eyes open and then sit up with a gasp.

I'm in Nate's room.

"It's OK." I glance up to see Nate sitting at his desk with a glass of water, his tousled hair sticking out at odd angles. "They left early this morning for meetings. Your door is closed, so they thought you were still asleep in there."

"Oh, good," I reply. I realize my nightgown is riding dangerously high on my thigh and pull up the sheet self-consciously.

"Coffee," Nate says, pointing to the bedside table next to me. I glance over and see he's placed a steaming cup there. "Cream and one sugar, right?"

"Yeah, thanks," I reply, reaching for it.

"Sorry about last night. I don't remember anything after I got home."

I smile even though I'm disappointed that he doesn't remember the kiss. "You were drunk, and just asked me to stay here for a bit. I didn't mean to fall asleep." I glance at the clock. "Shit, it's almost eleven? I never sleep that late."

"I didn't get up 'til nine—that's late for me."

My mind quickly returns to my concerns from last night. "I—I know you don't like to talk about this, but your mom—"

"What about her?" he says, already sounding defensive. I need to tread carefully.

"I know that it's painful to talk about, I just wanted to know: why did she leave?"

Nate crosses his arms over his chest. "Eileen left because she couldn't handle being a mother."

"What do you mean? How so?"

"I was out of control when I was a kid, and she couldn't handle it. Couldn't handle me."

"That's what your dad told you."

"That's what happened," Nate replies, frowning at me. "I still remember the night she left. They went out for dinner, and I stayed home with a babysitter. One of many, because I kept driving them away, and I misbehaved again. I threw a tantrum, broke a glass…I'm pretty sure the babysitter quit as soon as my parents got home. Anyway, they got in this big fight—I could hear it even in my bedroom—and the next day she left."

"And you've never seen her again?"

"In court a couple times. But after that, she wasn't really interested in seeing me. She tries to call here sometimes, maybe she feels guilty. She always tries to blame my dad for what went down," he adds bitterly.

"Did you think that if…if you had been better, she wouldn't have left?"

He shrugs. "Doesn't matter now. Why are you asking about this stuff? Did I talk about it when I was drunk or something?"

"No, no." I put my coffee down on the nightstand. "She called here last night."

"Eileen? You *talked* to her?"

"Well, yeah, she was really upset."

"Fuck, Brynn," he swears, standing up. "Why would you do that? This has nothing to do with you."

"I was just trying to help…"

"I don't need your help," he spits at me.

"Would you just listen for a second?! She called because she thought you might be willing to listen to her after what the woman said on the TV show—"

"What are you talking about?" he growls.

"She said your dad was cheating on her, that's why she left. Nothing to do with you."

"Get out," he says, raising his voice and pointing to the door.

"Nate, my dad left, too, OK? I know what it's like. But she sounded so lost, she's desperate to talk to you. I'd kill for my dad to sound like that about me."

"Oh, so that's what this is about, *your* daddy issues."

"No! That's not what I meant," I plead, his words stinging to my core.

"Look, I'm sorry that your dad isn't around, but your whole situation has nothing to do with mine!"

"Fine!" I shout, feeling hurt. I push off the sheets and stand up. "I promised her I'd tell you, so I did. I'll never try to help you again."

"That's all I ask!" he calls after me as I stomp out of his room.

I slam my bedroom door behind me, my fists balled in anger. I walk straight to my bed and grab my pillow and swing it down as hard as I can onto the mattress. *I. Can't. Believe. I. Ever. Had. Feelings. For. That. Asshole.* I think as I bring the pillow down again and again until I'm out of breath.

It's officially time for me to move on.

CHAPTER FIFTEEN

* * *

"You look nice," my mom says as I enter the kitchen, giving me a wink.

"Mom…" I reply, rolling my eyes.

"Well, you do! Where are you two going tonight?"

"La Mirabelle."

"French—how romantic!"

"It's just a first date, OK? Don't get too excited." I turn as Nate and Pierce enter from the dining room.

"I just have a good feeling about this one, that's all." She continues, pouring me a glass of water, "And he's picking you up, right?"

"Oh, do you have a date tonight, Brynn?" Pierce asks, wiggling his eyebrows at my mother.

"Yes," I groan, not wanting to make a big deal out of it.

"Greg! The intern from your office," my mom tells him.

"Well, well. You know, I remember seeing you two huddled together in the copy room last week, and thinking to myself, 'those two would make a fine couple.'"

I blush as my mom smiles enthusiastically. It's amazing how quickly things have gotten back to normal after that woman went on TV. For about a week, a handful of photographers waited around outside the gate, but they eventually left when the buzz died down. Pierce told us he has investigators working to discredit the woman's claims, and that everything will be back to normal. As for Nate and me…

"So it'll just be the three of us for dinner then," my mom chirps.

"Two, actually. I'm going out tonight, as well," Nate replies casually. I manage to resist the urge to look at him.

"Oh?" my mom asks.

"Nate, you should've let Holly know about your plans. How many times have I had this conversation with you? Responsibility, responsibility, responsibility," Pierce says as he crosses to the fridge. I glance at my mom, but she's looking down at her chopping board.

"Sorry, Holly," Nate says dutifully.

"It's alright, really," my mom says quietly. Thankfully, the doorbell rings and I can excuse myself. Angry as I am at Nate, I still don't like to hear his dad speak to him in such a condescending way.

I walk down the hallway to the foyer, and hear my mom and Pierce following me. I wince. I was hoping I'd get out the door without them all meeting—wishful thinking, clearly. I smile at Greg as I open the door. He's wearing a navy blazer and khakis, and looks a little nervous.

"Hey, Greg," I greet him.

"Greg! It's so nice to meet you," my mom says from behind me, forcing me to open the door all the way.

"Good to see you," Pierce says, shaking his hand.

"Mr. Thornhill," Greg replies formally. I see Nate appear in the entrance to the living room, leaning casually on the doorjamb but saying nothing. He smiles at me as I catch his eye. I frown at him and look away.

"Have her home by ten," Pierce instructs Greg.

"Yes, sir," Greg replies.

Pierce slaps him on the back just as I'm about to protest. "Don't worry, Greg, I'm just giving you a hard time."

"Oh, you had me for a second there," Greg says, exhaling in relief.

"Well, we should get going," I cut in so that Pierce doesn't have the chance to make any more *hilarious* jokes. "See you later!" I call, pulling the door closed behind me. I just catch Nate's smirking expression before I shut the door.

"You alright?" Greg asks as we walk to his car.

I force a smile and nod my head. "Yes, sorry! My mind wandered for a second. So, have you ever been to this restaurant before?"

Greg chose a very nice French restaurant for our date, it's a cozy, softly lit place set in the hills of Potomac. The wait staff is clearly passionate about their food, and delighted to have a young couple on a date that they can fawn over.

"So, how is it working for your stepdad?" Greg asks with a grin.

"You know, it's not that bad. I hardly ever think twice about it, really. He's all the way at the top of the company, and I'm all the way at the bottom, so we rarely interact on a day-to-day basis."

"Speaking of being at the bottom, Roderick called me Steven yesterday," Greg says, referencing Pierce's business partner.

I laugh. "No! Is there even a Steven working there?"

"Nope! That's the worst part. Who knows who he was thinking of…" He shakes his head remorsefully. "How come Pierce's son isn't working at Thornhill and Co.? Didn't want to work with his dad?"

"Um, the opposite, actually. Pierce is pretty hard on Nate...I feel kind of guilty about the whole thing because I think Nate wanted the internship, and then Pierce offered it to me to punish him. I tried not to accept, but Pierce insisted, and we'd just met, you know? I didn't want to be rude. Not to mention, my mom and Pierce haven't known each other for very long, so I was a little taken aback by how quickly they'd gotten married…" I bite my lip. "Sorry, wow. I'm rambling."

"It's OK, I get it. My parents are divorced, too."

"Well, mine aren't actually divorced. They weren't married in the first place," I clarify. But Greg isn't listening—he's squinting at the entrance to the restaurant.

"Speaking of…isn't that Nate now? Did you tell him we were coming here?"

"No, what? It can't be him," I reply, turning around to look. But sure enough, there he is, with a brunette stunner on his arm. That asshole! There's no way this is a coincidence—he must have overheard me telling my mom that Greg was taking me here.

"Brynn!" Nate says with a smile, leading his date over as the hostess trails them. "I didn't know you guys were coming here too! Greg, right? I'm Nate."

"Good to meet you," Greg says, shaking his outstretched hand.

"And this is Sophie," Nate adds, indicating his date.

"Hey," she says, glancing up for a moment from the cellphone in her hands.

"Did you all want to sit together?" the hostess asks. "We could pull another table over."

I could kill her.

"What do you think?" Nate asks Greg, his grin at full-wattage.

"Um, yeah, sure, why not?" Greg complies. I quickly stand and make my way over to Greg as a waiter helps the hostess pull another small table over. I'm not going to sit next to Nate and risk a repeat of that thigh-touching incident.

"I'll let you two sit next to each other," I explain with a saccharine smile as I take a seat next to Greg.

"We just ordered so you're not too far behind," Greg says as the hostess hands Nate and Sophie menus.

"Could we get a bottle of Dom for the table?" Nate asks the waiter, who nods happily and scurries off.

"Oh, you don't have to—" Greg begins.

"No, I insist. We're interrupting your date here," Nate replies magnanimously.

"I love champagne," Sophie pipes up, finally putting her phone away. I narrow my eyes at Nate and he studiously avoids my gaze.

"So, what were you two lovebirds talking about before we got here?" Nate asks Greg.

"Nothing, really," Greg replies glancing at me.

"You know, with your light hair, you two could almost be related. Cousins, maybe," Nate observes, leaning back in his chair. I swiftly kick his shin under the table. I see his jaw tighten but he doesn't even make a sound.

"Oh my god, totally!" Sophie agrees. "I made out with my cousin once, but I didn't know he was my cousin at the time. But then it happened again…"

I glare at Nate as Sophie launches into her story, and he smiles back at me. It's going to be a long night.

CHAPTER SIXTEEN

* * *

I spin around in Nate's desk chair as he shuts his bedroom door behind him. I've been waiting here, fuming, ever since Greg dropped me off twenty minutes ago.

"Jesus! What are you, a Bond villain?" he asks, genuinely startled.

"What were you thinking?! I know you did that on purpose to ruin my date, you fucker!"

Nate shrugs. "Come on, you really going to tell me you were having a great time before I got there?"

"Oh, so you were just helping me out, is that it? Greg was completely weirded out by the whole thing."

"Sophie had a nice time."

"Sophie, please! Where'd you find her? A high school dance?"

"I like her," he says with a smug grin as he sits on his bed.

"Oh, really? So why aren't you with her right now? Couldn't seal the deal?"

His smile falters a bit. "Maybe I didn't feel like it."

"Well, I guess there's a first time for everything. Just stay out of my life, OK?" I say, and stalk toward the door.

"I'll stay out of yours if you stay out of mine," he counters.

I turn to face him, "Is that what this is about? You're mad because I told you your mom called, so you try to ruin my date?" I hold out my hands in surrender.

"No, it wasn't that."

"Then what? I don't have time to play games with a crazy man-child."

"I'm sorry, alright? I just didn't like seeing you with that guy…something about his face is just, so punch-able," he says, standing up and walking over to me.

"Why? This is the second time you've come between me and a guy." I hold up a hand to stop him from protesting. "And yeah, I know, Jackson wasn't a good choice, but that's not the case with Greg, OK? He's a nice guy. So tell me, why do you care?" I challenge him as he looks down at me. There's a long pause as his pupils dilate, I can practically feel him struggling with the truth, but I refuse to move until he admits it.

"You know why," he says, looking me in the eye, his voice low and husky. Before I know what's happening, his arms are around me, pulling me against him. His urgency takes my breath away—his fingers reach desperately under my shirt, grabbing at my bra strap and expertly undoing the clasps. His mouth devours mine as he reaches back around my waist and picks me up effortlessly, bringing me over to his bed. As Nate puts me down, I realize my bra is hanging free in the back, and he breaks away from our kiss to rip off my top. He pauses to look down at my breasts curving out of my limp bra before diving into my neck. "Oh god, Brynn, I have to have you," he groans.

I gasp as he sinks his teeth into my skin and then flicks his tongue across my taut neck muscles on his way up to my ear. My knees buckle as his tongue presses into my ear, and I grab onto his neck for support. My mind can't keep up with what's happening, all my thoughts are a blur, but my body is urging me on, desperately.

As he sucks on my earlobe, I slide my hands down and under his shirt, finally feeling the body I've coveted for so long. His abs are even harder than I thought they would be, and they flex under my soft fingertips. I keep sliding my hands upward, feeling his nipples harden under my palms, and I feel the growing bulge of his cock pressing against my thigh…

I turn Nate Thornhill on. Holy fuck.

The thought drives me crazy and I feel myself instantly become moist with wanting, my body overcome with illicit, sinful lust. No man has ever made me feel this way before.

He steps back for a moment and pulls off his shirt, tossing it carelessly on the ground, revealing his incredible body for all its glory. Thousands of hours spent at the gym on and on the field have painstakingly sculpted his muscles into a fucking masterpiece for womankind. He slowly reaches forward and takes my bra straps under his expert fingers, pulling them off my arms and tossing my bra onto the pile of clothes on the floor. I shiver involuntarily as he looks down my exposed body, exhaling softly out of his mouth. He sinks to his knees in front of me and leans forward, kissing me gently on my stomach. I place my hands on his shoulders as he moves up, running his tongue underneath the crease of my breasts. I cry out as he takes my right breast into his mouth, sucking hard on my nipple. He brings one hand up to massage my left breast, and I dip my head back, feeling pleasure swell in my body like I never have before.

I feel his fingers hook over the top of my skirt and slowly pull it down as his mouth moves to my left breast, softly biting it before flicking his tongue back and forth across my areola. I hear my skirt fall to the floor and his hands glide up my legs from my knees, his thumbs hooking around my inner thigh. He dips his head and kisses me softly just above the top of my white cotton underwear.

"I've been dreaming about how sweet you taste," he murmurs, almost inaudibly. He pulls my panties down just a bit and runs his tongue over the now exposed skin. I begin to shake, a mixture of unbridled desire and nerves, as he slides my underwear down to my ankles.

I feel his warm breath on my skin, just a moment before his mouth is on me, kissing and licking my most intimate of places. I moan involuntarily at the sensation…it's completely new to me, and it feels better than I ever could have imagined. He flicks his tongue across my aching clit, sending jolts of rapture through every inch of me. With one hand I tighten my grip on his strong shoulders, digging my fingers into his hair with the other, and letting my head dip back in utter bliss as he licks my pussy with slow, strong strokes.

"Oh my god, Nate…" I hear myself moan from far away as I'm carried off by wave after wave of pleasure. Before I know what's happening, my body spasms, and I feel Nate grab my ass to keep me upright and pressed against his skillful mouth.

As I begin to come down, I feel his licks becoming gentler. He reaches up and puts his finger to my lips, and I instinctively take it into my mouth, licking and sucking his finger, thinking about how incredible it would feel to do this to another part of him…

He pulls his finger out of my mouth and slips it carefully inside my tight pussy. He circles it around slowly, and I can hear him grunt in satisfaction at my wetness. My eyes begin to open slowly and I glance down at him. He catches my eye and stands up, dipping his head down and catching me in a kiss, his finger still inside me. My eyes widen as I taste myself on his lips and he pushes his tongue inside me with abandon.

"I'm going to make you feel so fucking good," he promises with a wicked smile, undoing his belt buckle and unzipping his pants in one fluid motion before pushing them and his boxers to the ground. I gape at his massive cock as it's unsheathed from his underwear. Its size snaps me back to the reality of what's about to happen, and I feel overcome with fear and adrenalin…but I can't take my eyes off it. I want to feel him inside of me so much, but I think there's one thing I need to tell him first.

He bites his lip and moves against me again. I can feel his cock, throbbing and ready, against my stomach. He wraps his arms around me, and eases me back onto the bed and lays on top of me, kissing my neck.

"Nate…I…I have to tell you…" I murmur, his mouth a complete distraction.

"Mmm, whatever it is, it doesn't matter now," he replies, biting my earlobe.

"It might, though. I just thought I should tell you, or warn you maybe, in case I'm not very good—"

"I doubt that—"

"I'm a virgin."

I feel his body stiffen as the words cross my lips. He pulls back and looks me in the eye.

"What? No. No way."

I nod. "But it's OK. I want to do this."

"How…how are you a virgin?"

Oh, dear. This is not the kind of conversation I want to have right now. "I don't know, I just am. It just hasn't happened yet, but I'm ready now." I assure him.

"But you've…you must have done some things…" he begins worriedly.

"Yeah, sure, you know, kissing…"

"And? Wait, was that the first time anyone's ever gone down on you?"

I can only shrug. "I didn't think it would be that big of a deal. I just was telling you, in case I'm not that good, or if I bleed or something."

He rolls off of me and sits up. Shit.

"Brynn, it is a big deal, it's a very big deal to *me*."

"I don't understand…" I reply, sitting up and pulling the sheet over to cover me, suddenly feeling very self-conscious.

"It's just, your first time…it's going to mean a lot to you."

"So?" I say, confused. He spreads his hands open on his legs but doesn't say anything. I feel a sensation like a rock sinking to the bottom of my stomach. "Oh…you're saying it will mean a lot to *me*, but it won't mean a lot to *you*."

I stare straight forward as he turns to me. "Brynn, you're smart, gorgeous, funny, ambitious…you're wonderful…but like I told you before, I don't lie to women and say that I'm interested in something more when I'm not."

"I guess I forgot about your policy," I reply flatly, feeling like the biggest idiot in the world. The biggest *naked* idiot in the world. "Could you…could you close your eyes?"

"Brynn, I've seen—"

"Just close them, OK?" I glance at him to make sure he's complied, and then stand up and begin to gather my clothes from the floor. I slip everything back on as quickly as I can, and then look back at him. His eyes are closed, and he's sitting nude and perfectly still on the edge of the bed. He looks as perfect as I've ever seen him look, which is really saying something. My heart breaks a little, as I move to the door and shut it behind me.

I hurry down the hall and into my own bedroom, which now feels cold and empty. I crawl into bed without bothering to take off my clothes and pull the covers over me. I'm no different to Nate Thornhill than any of the other girls he's been with, and I should have known that. *Stupid, stupid, stupid.*

I hear a soft knock at the door and pull the covers up a little higher, but don't answer. If it's my mom, I don't want to see her, and if it's Nate, I really don't want to see him. There's another knock, a little louder, and then the door is slowly pushed open. I can just see Nate's shadow in the moonlight. He closes the door behind him and moves into the room. To my surprise, he walks around the foot of my bed and to the other side, then hops on, lying down over the covers next to me.

"I'm sorry," he whispers, laying his hands over his stomach.

"You don't have to apologize. You were just being honest."

"No, I think I do. And I'll stop interfering with you and other guys."

I clear my throat to keep the pain down. "Good."

"I don't really have female friends…" He says.

"Dana?"

"Dana and I are, well, fuck buddies, mostly. And that's what she wants, too, so it's OK."

"Mmm."

"But I'd…I'd like us to be friends."

"We're already step-siblings," I point out.

I can hear him smile next to me. "True. But that wasn't by choice." He pauses. "I like you. I can't deny that I'm attracted to you, of course, but I'm just not the relationship kind of guy. Not to mention the kind of issues that dating my own stepsister would bring up." He sighs. "So can we be friends?"

I consider for a moment. If I'm Nate's only female friend, then I really am different to him. Maybe not in the way I'd most like, but still, it's something.

"OK. Friends, then. Wait, actually," I turn onto my side and face him. "Before we're officially friends, I have to ask you some non-friend questions."

"OK…" he replies warily, turning on his side, too.

"Was I…am I…OK at all that stuff? You know…"

He laughs. "What we just did, you mean? Yes. You are more than OK at it."

I smile. "When did you lose your virginity?"

"When I was fourteen."

"Wow."

"She was my friend's older sister."

"Wow."

"How many women have you slept with?"

"Oh my god, I don't even know…"

"Wait, really? You don't even know?"

"I mean, dozens? I don't count."

"Sheesh. OK, one more: why aren't you the relationship kind of guy?"

He pauses. "I don't know," he says softly. "I tried a couple times, but that kind of closeness, it just makes me uncomfortable. That's all I know."

I nod, sensing he's telling me everything he can, and roll back over onto my back. I like the feeling of lying here with him next to me. I feel much more comfortable than I would have thought possible. I feel my eyes beginning to flutter closed as sleep pulls me under.

"Brynn...I..." I can just hear Nate say. "You're going to make some man very happy one day."

CHAPTER SEVENTEEN

* * *

"I'm just glad the whole thing has blown over," Greg says as we pull off the Beltway. I nod as I look out at the trees whizzing by in the dark. The woman who accused Pierce of sexual harassment rescinded her claims after it turned out she had accused two other former bosses of the same thing. "It just feels like there's been a shadow over the office for the last month."

"Yeah," I reply noncommittally.

Greg clears his throat as we near my house. "So, I'm glad we got the chance to go out again," he says.

"Me too," I reply with a smile. This is our third date, and he still hasn't tried anything. I'm wondering if tonight will be the night. A nervous silence falls over the car as we pull through the gates and onto the driveway. He stops in front of the house and then turns to me.

"Why don't I walk you to your door," he suggests.

"Sure." A few butterflies begin to fly around in my stomach. We undo our seat belts and hop out, meeting around the front of the car and walking up to the front door. I glance at him out of the corner of my eye and wish there were something calming I could say to him, because he looks way more nervous than I do. We reach the door and turn to each other.

"Well, goodnight," he says.

"Goodnight." He pauses, looking into my eyes, and then begins to move forward. I lean in, and close my eyes. His lips touch mine and I frown slightly. I mean, there's nothing wrong with his lips or anything, but I thought I'd feel…more. He keeps his mouth chastely pressed against mine for a few seconds and then pulls back and smiles at me.

"Goodnight, Brynn," he says again.

"Goodnight," I reply, and turn to go inside. I shut the door behind me, and lean back against it, disappointed. Greg and I get along well, and he's such a nice guy—I'd hoped I would eventually develop romantic feelings for him…but that kiss…was not so good. I sigh and continue through the foyer and into the kitchen.

"Hey," Nate greets me.

I stop as a buzz runs through me at just the sight of him. That's the feeling I can't manufacture when I'm with Greg. "Hey. You go for a run?" I ask, taking in his sweaty appearance.

"Yeah, well, just on the treadmill. Too dark for a trail run. Did you…did you have a nice time tonight?"

I glance over at him. He gulps a long sip from a Gatorade bottle and then puts it down on the counter.

"Um, yeah, it was good," I reply.

"I was just going to watch a movie in the den if you're interested."

"Fine, but I choose tonight," I reply with a smile. We've both committed to this whole being friends thing, though at times I feel like I'm going through the motions. I don't know if I'll ever be able to turn off the part of me that will always want more from him.

"No romantic comedies," he says, as he walks to the door of the kitchen. "I'm just going to hop in the shower really fast." The phone on the counter rings and he steps toward it, but it only rings once.

We both look toward Pierce's study as raised voices emanate from that direction. A moment later, we hear stomping coming our way and frown at each other in concern. Pierce storms in and walks to the fridge.

"Reporter?" Nate asks quietly.

"Your mother," Pierce replies, equally quietly, though there's a hint of venom in his voice. My eyes flick over to Nate. I hope I haven't made the situation worse by taking her call that one time. He meets my gaze and shakes his head quickly as though to warn me not to say anything. "I don't know how she got this new number—it's unlisted. That bitch just won't give up."

My mouth drops open at Pierce's language. I've never even heard him swear before, and it's so at odds with his genteel appearance that it sounds even more shocking coming out of his mouth.

"We're going to go watch a movie," I murmur, wanting to get away from him when he's in this kind of mood. I can feel the waves of anger coming off of him. But Pierce swings around to face Nate, the Gatorade bottle in his hand.

"How many fucking times have I told you to clean up after yourself?" he growls, and I shrink back.

"I wasn't done drinking—" Nate begins.

"Don't interrupt me! You think the rest of the world is just here to serve you? That everyone else exists to make your cushy life a little easier? You've never had to work for anything in your life. It's pathetic," Pierce spits at his son. I remain frozen on the other side of the counter, feeling like a coward, and not knowing what I should say.

I see color rise in Nate's cheeks, but all he says is, "Yes, sir."

With that, Pierce slams the bottle back on the counter and walks back toward his office without even looking at me. Nate remains motionless for a moment, then walks over to the bottle, drinks the rest of it, and tosses it into the recycling.

"I'm sorry, you didn't deserve—" I start, feeling horrified by the scene I just witnessed.

"You still want to watch that movie?" Nate asks, tilting his head toward me but not making eye contact.

"Yes," I whisper back, unsure of what else to do or say.

"OK, meet you in there in ten minutes," Nate says simply and walks out. I wait until I can hear him walking up the stairs before I move. I've never heard a father talk to his son like that before, and our old neighborhood wasn't exactly full of model families. And the way Nate's shoulders slumped as Pierce was speaking to him, it was like he agreed with what his father was saying about him.

I walk up the stairs to my room and change into my sweats, before heading back downstairs to make some popcorn—food always makes me feel better. As soon as it's finished popping, I head into the den to wait for Nate. Should I tell my mom about what Pierce just did? Would she even listen? She seems to have drunk the Pierce Kool-Aid pretty heavily by this point. And now that Pierce has been the victim of false allegations, it will be even harder for her to believe anything bad about him. I glance up, frowning, as Nate walks in and sits down on the couch next to me.

"I can tell by that expression on your face that you want to talk," he begins. I smile slightly, he knows me well. "But the stuff with my parents—it's off-limits, OK?"

But I need to tell him that those things Pierce said aren't true. "Just—"

"No, Brynn. I really want us to be able to keep hanging out. But if you keep bringing it up…"

I sigh. "Fine. I won't say anything. In exchange, though…" I walk to the wide bookcases full of DVD options.

"No romantic comedies!"

"Big Fish," I say, pulling out the case.

"Is that a romantic comedy?" he asks, narrowing his eyes suspiciously.

"Well, not really. There is romance in it, but it's more about a family," I explain, careful not to mention the predominant father-son themes. "Hey, friendships have to have some compromise," I add with a smile.

"OK, fine," he says, rolling his eyes. He takes a handful of popcorn and leans against one end of the couch as I pop the DVD in. As I make myself comfortable on the other end, he pulls a blanket from the back of the couch and arranges it over my feet, because he knows that they get cold.

I feel a pang in my chest at the small gesture, but try to push it away. He's not being romantic, just thoughtful. I look up at the large TV screen as the picture comes up. I feel more comfortable around Nate than I do with anyone else in my life right now, so I have to settle for being friends with him. Otherwise I could lose him altogether.

CHAPTER EIGHTEEN

* * *

"You and Nate head down there so we don't lose the reservation!" my mom instructs me. She planned a family outing to go rafting on the Potomac, but Pierce is stuck at the office in meetings, even though it's a Saturday. "I'll swing by and get him and meet you there."

"You sure?"

"Yeah, he said he'd only be a little longer," she assures me.

"OK," I reply with a shrug, and walk into the anteroom off the kitchen where Nate is slipping on his sneakers.

"My mom says they're going to meet us there," I tell him.

"Fuck it, let's make tracks, Sis." he smirks.

And off we go in his Wrangler, Nate blasting some god-awful metal music.

"How do you listen to this shit? It sounds like two cat's screwing in a trashcan." I shake my head.

"What? This is Slayer, they're classic trash metal, you have to have respect." He says reverently. "I always listen to *Reign in Blood* before all of my games."

"Lovely." I screw my face up in mock horror.

He turns it up louder, nodding his head enthusiastically as the guitar riffs collide into what I assume is his favorite part of the song. It's strange to see him let loose like this, and even though I think his taste in music is horrifying, I have to admit I like to see him enjoying himself.

Thankfully, the boathouse is just a little ways down the Potomac in the direction of the city, and I'm only subjected to Slayer for a few more minutes. The temperature on this August day is in the mid-nineties, but my mom was insistent upon doing a family activity outdoors. As we take a left on the dirt road with an old sign pointing the way, I spot an empty parking lot, and figure most people are wisely staying inside with their air-conditioning today.

After we park, Nate heads over to the wood-slatted structure to secure the boat, and I take the sunscreen out of my bag. As Nate walks back over, he smiles as he sees me struggling to smear it in between the straps of my sports bra.

"Want some help?" he asks.

"…Sure," I reply, though I'm anything but. The idea of Nate's hands on me, when I know nothing else is going to happen, sounds like torture. I might actually prefer getting a first-degree sunburn, but he's already taken the bottle from me and squeezing some of it out into his palm.

"Um, just pull the back of your shirt up," he instructs me. I do as he says, pulling it up to my hairline. I feel his greased-up hands slipping under the straps of my bra, and am glad he can't see the blush that immediately spreads across my face. I take a deep breath, trying to keep my raging hormones at bay, as his fingers slide around the side of my ribcage.

"Now you do me," he says, as I release my shirt.

"That's what she said," I mutter.

"Ha!" Nate barks, a short, joyful shout of laughter. "I didn't know you were funny Brynn," he says, grinning wide at me.

"There's a lot you don't know about me." I say, daring to meet his gaze for a brief moment.

I clear my throat and take the bottle of sunscreen from him, willing myself to keep my thoughts clean. He pauses, then turns around and pulls off his shirt. I groan inwardly at the sight of his wide, muscular back.

Where are our parents? I need some kind of buffer between us. But there are no signs of any cars pulling into the parking lot anytime soon, so I dutifully squeeze some lotion onto my fingers and then begin to spread it across his back. I carefully press it all the way up to his neck, across his shoulder blades—feeling the sinewy ropes of muscle there, down his back, and finally down to the top of his athletic shorts, my fingers venturing just inside his waistband. I hear him suck in a small bit of air, and see the slight throbbing of his member in his shorts. He's trying hard to hold back, I can tell.

"OK, all done!" I say overly cheerily, as I hand him the bottle. Nate tosses his shirt into the back of his Jeep and begins to spread sunscreen across his chest. I keep my eyes trained on the hazy river.

"They say how long they were going to be?"

"Nope, my mom just said—" I break off as I hear my phone start to ring in my purse on the front seat. "I bet that's her now. Hey, Mom," I greet her as I accept the call.

"Hey, honey."

"What's wrong?" I ask, immediately hearing stress in her voice.

"Oh, it's nothing, but Pierce won't be able to get out of the office long enough to go kayaking today. I'm just going to drive down to the office now, so at least he and I can have lunch together."

"OK, should we—"

"No, you two go kayaking and have fun, alright? We'll see you tonight for dinner."

"Oh, alright, if you're sure," I reply, wincing as I catch Nate watching me, his muscular torso gleaming in the sun. "Your dad got caught up in work stuff, and my mom's going to go meet him at the office for lunch, so they're not coming. They said we should still go if we want," I explain as I hang up.

"Since we're here," Nate says with a shrug. "You ever been kayaking here before?"

"Never been kayaking at all."

"Well, you'll love it," he replies, locking up his car.

"Says the captain of the UVA crew team." I smile.

In short order, we're pushing off the dock in a tandem kayak. With Nate's powerful oar strokes, we quickly clear the shallow, muddy water and head toward the open water. "You'll get the hang of it," Nate encourages me, and I turn around to smile sheepishly at him.

"I think I'm just holding you back, here," I laugh, trying to get the feeling of how to dip the oar in the water at the right time.

"Well, I have a lot more experience than you in a boat," he says. "We used to train for crew on the Potomac in high school, but we were a lot closer in to the city. We'd pass Georgetown, the Kennedy Center…You'd be amazed at the wildlife you can see out here, though," he tells me as he steers us upriver and into the current.

"I feel so far away from everything," I observe as the sounds of traffic are quickly covered up by the trees rising on either side of us.

"This land used to belong to a Native American tribe called the—"

"Piscataway," I finish reflexively.

"Damn, I keep forgetting my stepsister is a nerd," he says, and I can hear from his voice that he's grinning. "I won't even try to impress you with my passion for local history, then."

"No, come on, impress me," I tease him.

"I can't hold a candle," he feigns defeat. "You get better grades than me."

"Yeah, well, put me on two varsity teams and I think those grades might dip a little. I don't know how you do it. My friends Allison and Miriam tell me I spend too much time at the library—I barely have enough time for them. Not to mention, I'm not athletically gifted *at all*," I add, nodding to my ineffectual rowing. "So you've got me there."

"I met Allison on the 4th, right?"

"Right."

"But Miriam?"

"She's back home in Memphis for the summer. She's my other good friend; she and Allison room together."

"Why don't you live with them?" he asks, and I pause to listen to his oars dropping quietly into the water.

"Mm, I thought about it, but I like living alone. My mom can be…"

"What?" he prods me.

"I'm trying to think of a more flattering word for needy."

"You can say needy if you want. I won't tell."

"OK, she's really fucking needy," I reply, feeling like a weight has been lifted off my shoulders. I hardly ever talk about the more negative aspects of my relationship with my mom. "Honestly, a lot less so since she's met Pierce, though. Sometimes I just feel like I'm—"

"Her mom," he finishes for me.

I turn to face him, raising my eyebrows. "Is it obvious?" I ask worriedly. "I don't mean to sound resentful."

"You're allowed to feel however you want about her," he responds with a kind smile, and I turn back around. "At first I thought you were fragile," he says after a moment. "Like if I dropped you, you'd break. I think that's why…that's why I wanted to test you a little."

"You mean when you felt me up at dinner with our parents sitting across from us?"

He laughs. "I can't believe I did that, and I don't think I've ever apologized."

"No, you didn't, jerk."

"I am sorry."

"So, you don't think I'm fragile now?"

"No. I think you're one of the toughest people I've ever met. Look!" he says suddenly. I glance back toward him and follow where's he's pointing. "A great blue heron," he explains as I spot the huge bird with its wings spread, perched on a rock in the middle of the river. "That's how they dry their feathers after they dive for fish."

He stops rowing for a while as we watch it. Suddenly it pulls its wings in, gathers itself like a coil, and launches into the air. We watch it fly into the distant treetops before we begin paddling up the river again.

"Why are you interested in history?" I ask him.

"I like understanding why people behave the way they do," he explains quietly. I resist the urge to ask how this relates to his *own* history, trying to respect the boundaries he's put up.

"How's Greg?" he asks suddenly. I turn around and narrow my eyes at him.

"What? That's a friendly question," he says with a devilish grin.

"I…I don't want to talk about it," I reply, a little more huffily than I intend to.

"OK…so that either means really good or really bad."

"It's not *really* bad," I protest.

"Uh-oh."

I sigh. "It's just, there's no…you know…"

"Spark?"

"Exactly. I have to tell him soon—I don't want him to get hurt. Not that I think I'm breaking his heart or anything—"

"I saw the way he looks at you."

"Meaning?"

"He's falling fast. I'd tell him before he falls any further."

"I think you're exaggerating."

"Trust me."

We fall back into a comfortable silence as I think about his words. The stillness of the river, broken only by a soft wind blowing through the trees, helps to ease my anxiety over the conversation I need to have with Greg. The concept of "problems" seems to fade out here, though perhaps it's the unrelenting heat, which feels like it's beginning to melt my body into the seat of the kayak. I grab the sweating bottle of water from between my feet and take a long swig.

"Water?" I ask Nate, turning to offer it to him. He takes it, brushing my fingers with his as he wraps his long fingers around it. My insides clench…speaking of a spark. I spot a house very much like ours up on a hillside in the distance. "Where'd you live before the house now?"

"Townhouse in Georgetown." He says. "It was less of a behemoth. Had more character."

"The mansion isn't your taste?"

"It was always big for two people, and it still seems big, even for four. But what I really don't like is that it's got all these fake historical touches about it, and none of them are genuine."

"Anathema to a history major."

"Exactly. I always pictured myself in a smaller house, maybe a converted barn or something…one that was actually built in the time period it looks like it was built in. Maybe somewhere quieter than DC…it's pretty elitist here…I want my kids to grow up more modestly than I did."

"You want kids?" I ask, surprised.

"You don't?"

"No, I do…I'm just surprised. You know that having kids might necessitate being in a relationship with a woman for longer than you're used to."

He laughs. "I honestly hadn't thought of that. I always just pictured myself with kids. Is that horrible?"

"Yes!" I reply, quickly reaching down and flinging water back at him.

"Hey!" he cries, and grabs the sides of the kayak, beginning to rock it back and forth. "I'll tip this thing over," he warns me with a grin.

"Nate!" I protest, grabbing on. He relents, and keeps rowing after a moment.

"I think your mom picked the hottest day of the year," he observes.

"Want to head back?" I ask, hoping he'll say no.

He pauses. "Guess we should."

I nod, feeling disappointed, and dip my oar in the water to help him turn the kayak. Now that we're going with the current, it takes us much less time to make the return trip back to the boat house.

"How's your shoulder?" I ask.

"It's better, actually," he says happily, "thanks for asking."

I feel a tightening in my throat as we pull into the shallower water. Nate steps onto the dock first, then offers me his hand to help me get out of the unsteady boat.

"Much shadier under the trees," he observes, nodding to a hiking trail that cuts through the trees behind the boat house. I look at him questioningly. "Short hike before we go back?"

I nod and smile, trying not to look too pleased.

CHAPTER NINETEEN

* * *

"You've got good stamina for someone who doesn't do sports," Nate observes as our "short hike" goes into its second hour.

"I've been swimming in the pool pretty frequently, maybe that's it," I reply, though really I think it's that the conversation hasn't stopped. We're high over the Potomac now, on a dirt trail that winds around large boulders. He was right—it is cooler under the trees, but it's still just as humid.

"Is that it?" I ask, pointing to a three-leaved plant at the base of a tree.

After telling Nate that I manage to get poison ivy every other year, he's made it his mission to teach me how to identify the rash-causing the plant.

"Not red enough. By this time of the summer, it'll be more red and oily-looking. And the edges of the leaves are too jagged," he says as he bends over to look at it. A pair of female hikers approach us on the trail, headed the opposite direction. I watch them drink in Nate's shirtless, sweaty appearance and giggle to each other. As they pass, they smile flirtatiously at him, but he just politely smiles back before turning to me. "You're good at so many things, but identifying plant species…" he intones in a mock-serious voice as he shakes his head.

"Hey, if that's my weakness, I'll take it," I reply with a grin.

"Yep, poison ivy, that's your kryptonite," he teases me.

"What's yours? Intimacy?"

"Intimacy? How dare you! It's *commitment*. Very different."

"Oh, duh, of course. My apologies," I reply, glad we can joke about this kind of thing. "Wait, there!" I say, pointing to an ivy crawling up a tree trunk on the river side of the trail.

"Where? I don't see it," Nate replies, craning his neck.

"There!" I repeat, walking off the trail and into the underbrush.

"Brynn, be careful! And I don't think that's poison ivy, anyway."

"No, really! See, it's red—" I break off as I feel the ground beneath me give way. What I thought was solid earth was just an overhang of vegetation. My stomach flies into my throat as I begin to fall, the horizon instantly becoming a blur. I gasp and turn, frantically grabbing onto the dirt and branches nearby.

"Brynn!" Nate yells, and dives into the brush after me. I feel him grab my hand as I struggle to find a foothold on the steep hill beneath me. My feet frantically search for support and I begin to panic. "It's OK, it's OK, I've got you," Nate says. The steadiness in his voice causes me to look up at him. He's looking back down at me, his eyes sure and calm. I take a deep breath and reach my other hand up. He grabs it and begins to pull me up. "Under your right foot, there's a rock," he says, peering over the edge. "Don't look down, just feel for it. Just an inch to your left. Keep looking at me."

The expression in his eyes arrests me, and I still for a moment, then slowly begin to move my foot to the left. There. I feel my sneaker knock against it, and move my foot up and onto it.

"OK, now just push off and I'll pull you up. One, two, three!" I shove my foot down and he kneels and pulls me up and back onto him. I land squarely on top of him, shaking with fear and adrenaline. I feel his arms reach around me and squeeze, almost pressing the last of the air out of me.

"Fuck, Brynn," he whispers in my ear.

"Are you OK?" I reply, realizing he's landed on his back.

"Am *I* OK? Are you?" he says, sounding shocked.

"Um, I think so, though it's hard to tell right now."

"Oh, sorry. Here, stand up," he says, and I lean to the side of him. He jumps up then offers me both hands. I take them and stand, wincing as I put weight on my right foot. "What's wrong?"

"My ankle, I think."

"Let's get back on the trail where I can look at it." He takes my arm and wraps it around his shoulder. I feel his arm around my waist and I'm practically lifted off my feet as he walks me back onto the trail. He guides me down to a seated position and I lean back on my hands as he gently picks up my right foot. "It's a little swollen," he observes, "but I don't think it's broken—probably a bad sprain. Think you're OK to walk back if I help you?"

"Yeah, I'll be fine," I assure him. He helps me stand up and puts my arm around his shoulders. I take a deep breath as we take our awkward first steps back toward the boathouse, and I realize I'm in for a full hour of being pressed up against him. "You're really sweaty, you know that?" I say with a smile.

"Hey, you better be careful or I might lose my grip," he replies.

"How high up was I?"

"Probably best not to think about it."

"That's pretty high."

"Well, I'm glad you're alright…mostly."

I don't know if it's the scare from almost falling, or if we're both just tired, but the slow walk back takes place in almost silence. I wish I could think of something to say to break the tension, but having his shirtless body pressed up against me is too much. I can feel our sweat mingling together and our breath syncing along with the rhythm of our footsteps. As we finally sight the parking lot, he stops and moves in front of me, then bends over, looking back at me expectantly. I laugh and lift my bad leg up onto him, and then jump up as he hoists me the rest of the way. He walks with me on his back until we reach the car, then deposits me right next to the passenger side door.

As he jogs around to the driver's side, I turn to look around the parking lot. There are still only a few cars here, and in the corner is a blue sedan with a woman wearing sunglasses behind the wheel. I stare at her for a moment, because with her blonde hair, I thought for a moment that she was my mom. As we make eye contact she quickly looks away, and I hear the car start after a moment. Maybe she was just staring at Nate like the other women we encountered today. Or maybe she's a reporter…Pierce warned the family that there could still be a few hanging around.

"Are you OK to get in by yourself?" Nate asks, rolling down the window.

"Oh, yeah, sorry," I reply, snapping back to attention. I open the door and use my left leg to hop into the elevated seat.

"Everything alright?" he asks.

"Yeah, it's fine."

When we arrive back at the house, Nate basket-carries me straight from the car into the kitchen, gently setting me down on a chair in the breakfast nook. He kneels in front of me and unlaces my shoe, then slips it off and peels my sock off.

"Can you wiggle your toes?" I move them back and forth. "And now really slowly move your whole foot around." I wince as I circle it and pain shoots up through my leg. "I broke my ankle playing lacrosse my junior year, and I don't think that's what this is.

Let's ice and wrap it and see how it is tomorrow, or Monday. If it's still bad, I'll take you to the doctor."

"You know how to wrap it?"

"Hey, when it's not my own hand, I'm pretty good at it." I watch him take down that same first aid kit from the cabinet and set it down on the floor as he kneels in front of me again. He carefully wraps athletic tape around my ankle and then around the middle of my foot, hooking it around and around until my ankle is firmly stabilized. "OK, let's get you into the den so we can ice it."

I begin to stand but he bends over and scoops me up again, carrying me through the hallways to the cozy den. He sets me down on the couch and then disappears. I grab a pillow and set it behind my back as I stretch my legs out, marveling at the sudden appearance of Nate's caretaker instincts. He reappears with a Ziploc bag of crushed ice and a glass of water, setting the latter down on the table next to me before lowering the ice down onto my ankle. I shiver as he places it down, and he pulls the throw down from the back of the couch. He grabs one end and unfolds it, then sits on the edge of the couch next to me to lay it over me, tucking the corners in around my body.

I become very aware of my own breathing as he moves over me. I watch his hands as they take the edge of the blanket and tuck it around my shoulders. His right hand moves slowly from the blanket onto the exposed skin of my neck. I hold my breath as he lightly runs his fingertips up onto my jaw, then over to my chin. With his thumb and forefinger, he gently tilts my head up until I look at him. He's staring at my mouth, and only pauses for a moment before he bends down.

"Please don't," I whisper as he's just inches away from kissing me. "If you don't want anything more, it's just cruel."

"What if I do want something more?" he says, his dark blue eyes flicking up to mine.

"More…" I repeat, rolling the word around my tongue. "What kind of more?"

"I've never felt about someone the way I feel about you. I've tried fighting that feeling, I've tried reasoning with it, but it just keeps getting stronger. I have to give in—I need to. I can't tell you I know exactly what this will look like…I've never done anything like it. But I promise you that when I'm with you, I'll be with only you. And I want you to be with only me."

I stare up at him. That's still a lot of unknowns, but I sense that he's giving me everything he can right now. Plus my heart is about to beat out of my chest, and my resistance is giving out.

"Only you," I nod, before reaching around his neck and pulling him toward me. Our lips meet in an open kiss, our tongues finding each other's and mingling with desperate passion. He presses me back against the cushion, his hands grasping my waist over the blanket and quickly moving up and over my breasts. I arch my back into him, wanting to feel him against me…feel him everywhere.

"You guys home?" Nate jumps away as we hear my mom's voice from the foyer. He takes a deep breath and then runs his hand through his hair before responding.

"We're in the den!" he calls back, then turns to me. "Tonight," he murmurs, his eyes burning with promise.

CHAPTER TWENTY

* * *

"Are you OK, Brynn?" my mom asks me, frowning.

"Yeah, I'm fine," I reply lightly as I use my napkin to try to clean the tomato sauce off my shirt where I've just spilled it. Nate's promise of an evening rendezvous has left me clumsy and distracted throughout dinner. I had just finished cleaning up the glass of water I knocked off the table when I dropped a piece of chicken off my fork and onto my shirt.

"Sorry I couldn't make it today, guys," Pierce says. "Looks like you could have used some more supervision. Nate shouldn't have taken you on any dangerous trails."

"Oh, it wasn't dangerous," I rush to Nate's defense. "He was trying to teach me how to spot poison ivy, actually, and I walked right off the trail. I didn't realize how close I was to the edge and the ground just gave way under me. It was all my fault.

He was the one who pulled me back up and taped my ankle."

"Well, it couldn't hurt to get it looked at by a doctor on Monday," my mom points out.

"I think it'll be fine, really," I insist.

"Anyone want dessert?" my mom asks.

"No, thanks," Nate and I both respond at the same time. I bite my lip to keep from laughing.

"What's so amusing?" Pierce asks, looking at his son, his voice dangerously quiet.

"Inside joke," I reply quickly. "I'll help you clear the table, Mom." We both stand and grab a couple plates and head into the kitchen. As soon as the swinging door shuts behind me, I hear Pierce's voice. Even though his words are muffled, I can tell by his tone that he's berating Nate for something. I look at my mom. She turns on the water and begins rinsing off the plates before putting them into the dishwasher. "Is it OK with you that he talks to Nate like that?"

"It's between the two of them," my mom replies quietly without looking up at me.

I feel anger surge inside me. "You keep trying to make us a family, but then you won't get involved in their relationship. You can't have it both ways." Before she can reply, I spin back around and into the dining room. Pierce breaks off abruptly as I enter the room, and I quickly clear the rest of the dishes before limping upstairs to my room.

I take a deep breath as I close my bedroom door behind me. I don't want to have this night ruined by my anger at my mom and Pierce. I head into the bathroom and turn on my shower. I still haven't had a chance to wash off the sweat from our kayaking and hiking trip today, and I want to smell like a rose tonight.

My body tingles in anticipation as I peel off my shirt and shorts. I glance down at my wrapped ankle, wondering if it's OK to get wet. Probably fine. I pull off my sports bra and underwear and then study myself in the mirror, running my hands over my breasts and then across my stomach. Nate's already seen me naked, I remind myself, as nerves surge up in my stomach. And I already know he likes me. It will be OK.

I step under the hot stream of water and take my time washing my hair. As the conditioner sets, I shave my legs and my bikini line, going a little bit narrower than I would normally. I know that a lot of girls at college go completely bare, but I can't bring myself to go that far.

I turn off the water and towel myself off, then part my hair in the middle and let it air dry. I pull a pair of cotton pajama bottoms and a camisole from my bureau and put them on. I'm not sure if that's sexy or not, but I'm trying not to overthink it. I'm certainly not succeeding, but I am trying.

I head over to my computer and sit down. I know that Nate will probably wait for our parents to go to bed before he does anything, so I've got a couple of hours to go at least. I begin to click around the internet, but I'm not able to absorb myself in anything. I keep wondering what's going to happen tonight. I don't want to get my hopes up, but I think I have an idea. Or at least, I know what I *want* to happen. I finally decide to play some mindless TV on Hulu, and settle back in my chair.

"Goodnight, Brynn!" I finally hear my mom call as she heads up to the third floor. I freeze.

"Goodnight!" I call back, and immediately begin pulling at the ends of my hair. I keep watching TV until I hear Pierce heading upstairs, too, then quickly close my computer and hurry into the bathroom, wincing as I put too much weight on my right ankle. I run my fingers through my hair and decide I should brush my teeth. Just as I'm putting my toothbrush back down, I hear a soft knock at my door. My heart jumps in my chest.

I walk back into my bedroom just in time to see the door open and Nate stick his head in.

"Hi," I murmur.

"Hi," he replies, taking a couple more steps in and closing the door behind him. I smile at him nervously. I suddenly have no idea what to say—the usual ease of conversation between us is replaced with jittery nerves and excitement. His appearance right now isn't helping matters. He's barefoot, and wearing jeans and a v-neck white t-shirt. He looks impossibly, effortlessly sexy. "I can't remember the last time I was nervous with a woman," he finally says.

"Oh, well...good. I'm nervous, too, I mean."

He smiles and begins to walk slowly toward me. "I want to do everything with you, Brynn. The idea of being the first one to show you...everything..." He takes a deep breath. "But I'm going to go slowly. You have to tell me if I'm ever moving too quickly, alright? It's going to be hard for me not to get caught up in the moment."

I nod and realize that I've been holding my breath while he's been talking. He stops just in front of me and wraps his arms around my waist, then leans his head forward until his forehead rests against mine.

"Come to bed," he whispers. A thrill of pleasure runs through me.

"You don't know how long I've wanted to hear you say that." He grins widely and presses his lips against mine. In contrast to our recent urgent caresses, this one is slow and gentle. Perhaps because we know we're finally on the same page, and we have all night to spend with each other. His tongue delicately flicks against mine, and I feel his hands move under my ass and pick me up. He spins and walks to the bed, setting me down in a seated position on the edge. "Is there anything...*in particular* you want tonight?"

"I just want you," I reply with a shrug.

"Well, that I can do." He grabs the bottom of his t-shirt and pulls it off over his head. I bite my lip. The tightness and size of his muscles always takes me aback. I lean forward and nuzzle my nose into the hair just under his belly button, then softly kiss him. I hear a low grunt from the back of his throat and lean back to look at him questioningly. He's looking down at me like he's about to devour me in one bite, but he takes a deep breath and kneels down in front of me, spreading my knees apart so he can push right up against me. He pulls me toward him and opens my lips with his.

As our tongues meet, I feel his fingertips gliding softly over the top of my camisole, barely touching my right breast. I press forward into his hand, but he pulls back. I quickly learn my lesson and stay still as his fingers return, teasingly running just under the fabric. Finally I feel him reach up with both hands and pull the cotton down and hook it under my breasts so it stays put.

He dips his head and pulls my breasts together, taking one nipple into his mouth and sucking on it, then quickly moving over to the other. I moan and tilt my head back as my hands grip the comforter beside me. He backs off and takes the bottom hem of my shirt, pulling it off over my head.

"You have the most gorgeous breasts," he breathes, palming them as though he's sculpting clay.

"Really? I've always been self-conscious of them."

"Why?" He looks at me in shock. "They're perfect." He leans forward to kiss me softly, then begins to unbutton his jeans.

"Wait, um, can I?" I stop him. He smiles at me and stands. I slowly reach forward and finish unbuttoning them, then move the zipper down. I can feel his eyes on me, but I keep my gaze on what I know is waiting for me underneath his denim. The arch of his cock is pressing against his boxer-briefs as I push his jeans past his knees. I pause and then take the sides of his waistband and pull them out and around. His thick mushroom tip springs out as soon I pull the boxers down. He's so big that I can't begin to imagine how he's going to fit inside me.

My worry must read on my face, because he says, "We'll take it slow." I nod and push the boxers down to his jeans, holding them as he steps out of them. I gulp as I'm face-to-face again with his manhood. "Have you ever…?" he asks leadingly, nodding down at himself.

"Never," I reply.

"Give me your hands." I obey, reaching up to place mine in his large outstretched palms. He places one on his thigh, and brings the other to his shaft. He wraps it around the base, and then moves it up to his tip, then back down. "Just like that. Nice and easy at first." He removes his hand and I keep going, feeling the soft, veiny skin of his cock ripple slightly at my touch. He takes my other hand and places it on his balls, massaging them with me. His hands then drop by his sides, and I look up to see his eyes closing and his lips parting.

Instinctively, I lean forward and, tucking my lips over my teeth, I take him inside my mouth. I hear him gasp and I smile inwardly. He doesn't know that I've read my fair share of dirty books, even if I've never actually put anything into practice. I keep moving my mouth down his length, seeing how far in I can take him. I stop when he hits the back wall of my mouth, though I'm still not at his base, and then begin to slide back out.

"Oh, fuck, Brynn. You sure you've never done this before?" he asks me, eyes wide as I swirl my tongue around his tip and then pull him back inside my mouth. I move my hand back to his balls and massage him again as I move up and down his dick. I hear him moan and feel his hand move to the back of my head, his fingers grasping my hair. "Enough," he grunts, pulling his hips back. "Stand up."

Normally when Nate takes that tone with me or orders me around, it really gets under my skin. But right now, it's turning me the hell on. I jump to my feet. He abruptly takes the elastic waist of my pants and yanks them to the ground. We stand facing each other naked, the air between us charged. Without taking his eyes off mine, he reaches forward and between my legs. I cry out softly as he slips one finger over my wet clit, and then inside me. I almost fall forward at the strength of my reaction to his touch, and have to grab onto his shoulders to support myself. He pulls me into him so that I'm curled against his chest, my head resting just under his chin.

His finger moves in and out of me, and his thumb flicks over my clit. I reach down and begin to run my hand up and down his cock like he showed me, though I'm so turned on that I'm hardly aware of what I'm doing.

"You're almost ready," he whispers. He pulls his hand out of me and picks me up under the armpits and tosses me onto the bed. In a second he's pushing my legs apart and kneeling between them. His head ducks down and I buck wildly as his tongue takes a long lick of my clit. I feel him slip two fingers inside me, and can feel him pressing them all around, stretching me out. His tongue circles and flicks against me the whole time, until I begin to unravel.

"Oh, Nate, oh, yes!" I cry out, but he stops. I gasp at the sudden lack of contact and pick up my head to look at him. He's no longer between my legs, but standing to get something out of his jeans. He smiles at me as he shows me the condoms he's taking out of his pocket. He rips one off and pulls it open with his teeth, then tosses the rest on the bed next to me as he walks back. I watch as he holds it to his tip and then unrolls it down his shaft. Then he kneels back on the bed, his legs between mine, and lies down on top of me with his weight on his elbows.

"This first time will probably hurt a little, but it'll feel good soon," he promises, brushing a strand of hair behind my ear. I nod nervously. He kisses me, his tongue softly caressing mine, as I feel his dick against my opening. I can't believe it's finally happening. He reaches down, pulling my leg up and holding it against his hip as he takes his cock in his other hand, positioning it at just the right angle.

I gasp as he enters me and sharp pain reverberates through my entire lower half. I feel his hips stop their forward motion. He moves his mouth over to my ear, softly sucking on my earlobe and darting his tongue in and out as he moves forward again. The pleasurable sensation at my ear helps to distract me from the massive pressure I feel pressing into me. I close my eyes and wrap my arms around his back, willing myself to relax. I know I'm in good hands. Just when I think the pain will be more than I can handle, he stops, and I can feel the skin around his hips pressing against mine. He's all the way in. He circles around slowly, and I feel my first twinge of pleasure at the sensation.

He pulls his head back and looks at me. "OK?" he asks. I nod, feeling breathless. Without taking his eyes off me, he begins to pull back out, all the way to his tip, before sliding in again. He pulls out a second time, and as he returns, my lips part in surprise at my body's response. I think he can sense that I'm starting to warm to the sensation, because he begins to move a little faster.

"Oh, Nate, that feels…it feels…" I trail off. There are no words. I simply wrap my legs around his back and dig my hands into his hair as he moves against me, as exquisite waves flow through my body. His lips find mine again, kissing me with a passion that matches the faster pace he's setting.

I feel an orgasm begin to build inside me. I've had orgasms before, including an amazing one with Nate, but this one feels different. It's so powerful that it scares me. I bear down against it, holding my breath to keep it at bay. But everything Nate is doing is working against me. I feel his hands move to my breasts, and my back arches against the heat of his palms. He kisses my neck as I bend to him, and his cock finds new and untouched nerve endings to drive me to the edge.

"Oh, Nate, it's too much…" I breathe, opening my eyes. "I don't know if I can." He slows down for a moment.

"Brynn, you're safe with me," he murmurs, his dark eyes finding mine, tenderness and passion mixed in them. "You just have to let go. Let go with me."

He begins to speed up, but his eyes don't leave mine. I follow his advice, trying to let the orgasm take me rather than trying to control it. "Yes, yes, Brynn," he grunts as my eyes roll back in my head.

He slams his hips into me now, driving his cock inside me. I hear myself begin to moan as though I'm outside of my own body. His torso lifts off of me and he thrusts in a little deeper. The slightly new angle is enough to push me right over the edge. I completely lose control, my body arching with spasms of its own accord. I can vaguely feel him bucking on top of me, his sweat dripping down onto my skin.

He collapses on top of me and I tuck my face into his neck. His body weight feels exactly right on top of me. I feel like I could stay like this forever.

CHAPTER TWENTY-ONE

* * *

I wake up to soft kisses on my cheek. My eyes flutter open in surprise.

"Mmm?" I murmur incoherently.

"You passed out," I hear Nate whisper back. I realize he's still on top of me—and inside me.

"Oh, sorry," I smile, blushing a bit. "I hope I didn't make too much noise."

He grins. "Well, I think if they'd heard anything, we would have known about it by now."

"How long was I asleep for?"

"Just twenty minutes or so. I was worried I was going to crush you." He kisses my lips and then reaches down. I watch him hold the base of the condom as he pulls out of me. The sensation of him leaving my body is jarring, and I lay still for another minute, absorbing it, as he walks to the bathroom. He comes back with a couple of wet tissues and I sit up to take them from him.

"It's OK," he says. "Lie back." I obey, and feel him carefully wiping up the inside of my thigh, and then begin to giggle. He stops and looks at me with a confused frown.

"I'm sorry, I just—I never thought I'd be in this position with Nate Thornhill!" I explain. He shakes his head with a bemused grin as I continue to giggle.

"You bled a little, but it didn't get on the comforter. That would have been tough to explain," he says as he returns to the bathroom.

"I could have just said I had my period," I point out as I pull my comforter back and crawl underneath the sheets.

"Oh, I guess that's true," he says, coming back and sliding into bed next to me.

"I can't believe I'm not a virgin anymore," I grin as he wraps his arms around me and pulls me close. "I was beginning to think it would never happen."

"So…you liked it?" he asks, running his fingers up and down my arm. I'm shocked to feel my body respond hungrily, as though I haven't just had a mind-blowing orgasm twenty minutes ago.

"Are you kidding me?" I ask, raising my eyebrows at him. "What about me? Was I…"

"You were excellent," he assures me. "It was different, though."

"Different, how?" I ask, frowning.

He shrugs. "I usually don't really know the girls I sleep with. Or have feelings for them. Even the ones I get to know, because we're hooking up regularly, I'll end it when they get too clingy."

A fissure of concern rises in my chest. "So…don't get clingy?"

"That wasn't a warning," he says, turning to me with a smile. "Besides, I don't think of you as clingy. Stubborn, maybe."

"Gee, thanks," I reply, rolling my eyes.

"So, why did it never happen? Losing your virginity?" he asks, turning to me and resting his head on his elbow.

"Well, I guess it's not that surprising. I've never really dated. My first kiss was with this guy David in my junior year of high school. It was really fast. And gross. His tongue just sort of darted in and out of my mouth. And then senior year, and freshman year of college, a few guys took me out, but it never really went anywhere. I mean, they were fine, but I really wanted to dedicate myself to studying, and getting a scholarship and all that."

"Did your mom put a lot of pressure on you to do well in school?"

I smile. "The opposite, actually. She was always begging me to get my head out of a book and put on some lip gloss. Which of course just made me want to stick my head even further into a book. I just never wanted to end up like her." Nate raises his eyebrows at me, and I sigh. "I mean, dependent on men. She never really learned how to do anything because she's so beautiful and charming and men would always do everything for her. But when I came along, they stopped coming around so much, and she had to take care of me all by herself. And even when they did, they'd eventually leave, and she'd be devastated. Curled up in bed for days, depressed, unable to care for herself…"

"So then you started taking care of her," he finishes. I nod. We settle back into the pillows for a minute. "Your mom should have known that not all books are created equal, though," Nate begins thoughtfully. "Some are far more interesting than others."

"What?" I ask, with absolutely no idea what he's talking about. With a devilish grin, he reaches over me and opens my bedside table. I shriek and grab his arm as I see his fingers graze over my copy of *Lady Chatterley's Lover.* But to my far more infinite horror, his hand keeps searching back and returns to the bed with my hot pink vibrator. "Oh my god, put that back!"

He ignores me, and studies it thoughtfully as my cheeks burn. "Someday I'd like to watch you use this on yourself," he comments. My mouth drops open and he glances up at me, his eyes boring into me. "What do you think about that?"

"I…I don't know," I whisper.

"Not tonight," he assures me, replacing the vibrator in the drawer and turning back to me.

"Tonight, I'll do all the work." I gasp as I feel his fingers slip between my legs and rub against my clit. "You have no idea how much it turns me on to be your first for all of this."

"Mmhm," I reply distractedly as my eyelids flutter. No way can I concentrate on speaking with his hand down there.

"Brynn, keep looking at me."

"Why?" I whine.

"Because I like to tease you," he replies simply. I bite my lip and turn my head back to him. His fingers rub my aching nub over and over again.

"I like it when you order me around," I whisper, feeling shocked to hear myself say such a thing out loud. His eyes widen.

"You do?"

"Only in bed," I explain. I watch his pupils dilate and his jaw muscles contract, as though he's struggling against some powerful reaction. He sucks in a breath of air and then blows it out of his mouth slowly.

"Oh, Brynn, there are so many things I want to do to you. But we can't just jump from zero to sixty." I nod in understanding and then moan as he slips a finger inside me. "You're so wet already. You want round two?" All I can do is moan in affirmation. "Turn around," he orders me, and a thrill of desire rushes through me. I obey, turning over onto my other side so that my back's to him.

He runs his hand over my ass and then back between my legs and inside me. I hear him fumbling with his other hand and then the sound of a condom being ripped open.

"Put your arms over your head," he tells me. I place them over my ears and onto the pillow, bending my elbows so that they don't hit the headboard. I feel his hand press down against my forearms, his long fingers easily reaching completely around me, and pinning me to the pillow. His other hand slides out of me and pulls my hips back toward him. I begin to tremble with anticipation, but don't have to wait very long.

I feel his cock at my slit, pushing into me as he holds me in place. I cry out from pain and pleasure as he reawakens the soreness he created the first time, but unlike that time, the pleasure is also instant and intense.

I feel his mouth at my ear. "You like that?"

"Yes, oh god, yes," I moan. He thrusts into me faster.

"It's so hard to hold back with you," he mutters, almost to himself.

"You don't have to," I reply. I hear him grunt in response and slam into me harder. Suddenly I feel myself being picked up and turned over. Before I know it, I'm on my hands and knees without Nate and me ever losing contact. I have to bite my lip to keep myself from screaming out in pleasure as he pulls out and drives back in. He's in so deep now, pressing directly against my g-spot with every thrust.

My body begins to shake with another orgasm and this time, I let myself go with it. I feel Nate's hands pulling my hips back to meet his with every thrust as he comes with me. My elbows collapse down with the final shudder of my orgasm, and Nate lands on top of me, immediately kissing the back of my neck.

"Oh, Brynn, I'm sorry," he murmurs, as he pulls my hair out of my face.

"Sorry? Why are you sorry?" I ask, befuddled.

"You're crying…I'm so sorry. I was too rough, I went too quickly, I—" he rushes on, sounding horrified.

My brain tries to catch up with him. "No, no. It didn't hurt. I didn't even realize I was crying. Everything felt amazing."

His body relaxes against mine. "I was so scared for a second there. I thought I hurt you."

"No, honestly…" I reach up to touch my face, and he's right—my cheeks are damp. "That's so strange. This doesn't happen a lot?"

He pulls himself up so he can look at me with an ironic grin. "I do try not to make girls cry, Brynn."

I laugh. "I'm sorry, I just meant…I wondered if this happens to other girls. I suppose I don't usually…you know, let go of control like that. Maybe the emotional release…"

"Maybe. Just as long as you're OK."

"I'm more than OK," I assure him.

"Sore?"

I nod. "A little."

"I'll get you some water," he says, kissing the back of my shoulder before gently pulling out of me. He comes back from the bathroom with a glass for me, and sits up in bed with me as I drink it.

"I wish you could sleep here," I murmur, resting my head on his shoulder. I feel spent, relaxed…and happy.

"Me too."

CHAPTER TWENTY-TWO

* * *

The next morning, I wake up reaching for Nate, but he's gone. I turn over onto my back in frustration. I thought that after we had sex my desire for him might fade a bit, become more manageable, but it's even stronger now. Even though I can feel a little soreness and pain between my legs, I want him to take me again, and again, and again.

I glance at the clock and am shocked to see it's almost noon. Well, I guess I did have a big day yesterday, between almost sliding down that cliff and losing my virginity. I slide under the sheets to the side of the bed and sit up on the edge. I roll my ankle and find that there's barely any pain, though I guess I should leave the tape on for one more day just to be safe.

I stand and pull on a pair of yoga pants and a t-shirt and head downstairs to the kitchen and fix myself some breakfast. My mom walks in just as I'm sitting down at the breakfast table.

"Wow, that's a lot of food, Brynn," she comments, raising her eyebrows at the amount of eggs and toast on my plate.

"Starving," I reply, pausing only momentarily then continuing to shovel food into my mouth.

"I can see that. How's your ankle?"

"Lot better." I clear my throat. I need to stop acting weird or my mom will know something's up. I put down my fork. "Did you have a nice lunch with Pierce yesterday? Where'd you go?"

"The Palm," she replies. "It was lovely. Pierce is a regular there and always gets the best table."

"Oh, good." I glance up as Nate slides opens the door from outside. He winks at me and I quickly bury my head back in my food so that my mom can't see the blush spreading across my cheeks.

"Just returning from your morning workout, Nate?" my mom asks as she begins to fix herself some tea. "You're both getting such late starts today."

"Must've been that hike," Nate replies nonchalantly. "How's your ankle?"

"Lot better," I repeat, holding it out from under the table and rolling it around to demonstrate.

"Better keep the tape on for another day just to be safe."

"That's just what I was thinking."

"Anybody want some coffee? I'm just putting some water on," my mom breaks in.

"Yes, please," we both chorus.

"You know, I'm so glad you two are getting along. That 'step' word has such a bad connotation, I suppose because of Cinderella…you know, the wicked stepsisters. But of course, having a bigger family can be such a positive thing," she muses, turning up the burner on the stovetop. I watch her for a moment, wondering if she's trying to bring up something about what I said to her last night, about how she needs to get involved in Pierce's harsh treatment of his son.

"Very positive," Nate replies seriously, not looking at me as I glare at him warningly. It is so not the time for one of his smartass comments.

"Pierce and I are going to the farmer's market in about an hour. You guys want to come?"

And miss a chance to be alone with Nate? "I was thinking I was just going to sit by the pool today," I reply. "Give my ankle a little more time to heal."

"Probably wise," my mom agrees. "What about you, Nate?"

"I have to, um…" he trails off, trying to come up with an excuse. "You know, I think my friend Jackson might swing by later, so I better stay home."

"OK, just the parents then," my mom with a faux sigh. Nate and my mom both leave the kitchen to take their coffee into other rooms, so I can finish off my breakfast in peace. After I clean up my plates, I decide to head into the den and turn on the TV. My body needs to digest that giant breakfast I just devoured.

Pierce and my mom find me sitting in there on their way out the door, and I wave goodbye. But as soon as the door closes, a ball of excitement forms in my stomach. I'm alone with Nate. I feel like a kid on Christmas morning. I push aside the throw and stand up, heading for the stairs and Nate's bedroom. A flurry of nerves hits me as I walk down the hallway and knock softly on his door.

"One sec!" he calls back. "OK, come in." I push the door open to find him standing just outside his bathroom, a white towel wrapped around his waist. He's dripping wet, having clearly just stepped out of the shower. "Oh, it's you," he says with a smile. I shut the door behind me.

"They just left."

"How are you feeling, really? I want to make sure I didn't go too fast last night. Any regrets?"

I walk toward him. "I do have one regret." He frowns in concern, his beautiful forehead marred by a line in between his eyebrows. "There was something I wanted to do last night, but I didn't get the chance." The tension immediately leaves his face.

"Which was?" he asks, the edge of his mouth twisting up in a questioning smile.

I reach forward and unwrap his towel in response, then kneel in front of him. I watch his cock grow hard in front of my eyes as he gazes down at me. Without another word, I run my hands up the front of his thighs, feeling his leg hair under my palms disappear as it reaches the line of his hips. I lean forward, trailing kisses just under his belly button. He smells amazing—a heady mixture of fresh shower combined with the very personal scent of his package. It's unlike anything I've smelled before, and though I haven't been with anyone else, I bet the smell is all his own.

I wrap my hands around the back of his thighs as I dip my head and kiss the base of his shaft. His cock jumps slightly in response to my touch, and I hear him groan. I wrap my hand around him, pulling him toward my mouth. I circle my tongue lightly around his tip, licking up a bead of liquid that has just appeared there.

I move to the base of his dick, pressing my tongue down hard as I make my way back up the underside of his shaft, then flick my tongue around his tip. Then I tuck my lips around my teeth and wrap them around him, stretching my mouth wide to receive him. I move slowly down his length, wanting to make him feel as good as he's been making me feel. And to tease him a little, too, if I'm being perfectly honest.

I look up at him as I pull back, and see him biting his lip as he looks down at me. I circle his tip with my tongue for a minute as he watches me. I feel myself growing wet—why going down on him turns me on so much I don't know, but it does. His fingers wrap around the back of my head, digging into my hair, as he dips his head back.

I take him in my mouth again and begin to move faster. I bring one hand up to massage his balls, and wrap the other around his shaft, following my mouth. I still can't fit his whole cock in my mouth, so I figure this is kind of a good cheat. My eyes begin to water a bit as I hear him begin to groan. I move even faster, excited to feel him come in my mouth, and to taste him.

"Oh, fuck, fuck, I'm coming," he moans, and suddenly my mouth is filled with liquid. I keep moving my head back and forth even as I feel it leak a little out of the corner of my mouth. Should I swallow it? I don't know what else to do, so I lean back for a moment and feel it run down my throat.

Nate's taking deep breaths above me, his chest heaving, so I lean forward again and kiss his shaft gently as it softens a bit. I guess I expected it to, you know, *go down* right away, but it stays mostly erect as I stand back up.

To my surprise, he wraps his arms around me and kisses me. I thought he might feel some compunction considering where my mouth has been, but his tongue slips readily against mine and I relax against him. His hand slides down my ass and he rubs himself against me.

"How much longer do you think they'll be gone?" he asks breaking away and bringing his other hand up to my cheek.

"No idea."

"Well, I'll make this quick, just in case." He pushes me away and steps back. "Strip."

I almost gasp at the pleasure his command sends rushing through me. I pull off my shirt and yoga pants, then unhook my bra and slide my panties to the ground as he watches. My lips part as he wraps his hand around his cock as it hardens completely again.

"I want you to go on birth control soon, OK? I don't want to have to wear a condom with you."

"Does it feel very different?"

"Oh yeah. And I want to feel myself right up against you." He walks over to his bedside table and pulls a condom out and tosses it on the bed. "Come," he says, holding his hand out to me. I walk over, and he turns me around, pulling my back against him. I feel his cock hitting the small of my back as he runs his fingers over my stomach and then up over my breasts, gently pinching my nipples. I groan into his touch. I've never felt anything close to the way he makes me feel.

"A little faster and harder this time, OK?" he asks, and I nod, already beyond speaking. His fingers slide down and over my clit, and I can hear the sounds of my wetness as he presses one finger inside me. "You're already so wet…good girl."

His other hand snakes up to my face and turns my cheek so that I'm facing him. He kisses me, hard, his tongue ravaging my mouth as his finger circles inside my opening. His thumb flicks over my clit and I cry out in pleasure and surprise. As if he were just waiting for this response, he turns me around and pushes me down on my back on the bed. He picks up the condom next to me and quickly rips it open and pulls it on. He grabs my hips and steps forward, pulling my ass down so that it's just on the edge of the bed. He bends over me, quickly pulling my breast into his mouth and gently nibbling on my nipple.

He moves his weight onto his elbows and I feel him pressing inside me. There's a slight soreness left over from last night, but also instant pleasure. He stretches me open, pushing slowly but surely until he's all the way in. My hands dig into his back as he thrusts again, a little harder. Then he stands up, still inside me, and pulls my legs up so that my calves are resting on his shoulders.

He moves his right hand over my crotch, and I moan as he begins to circle my clit with his thumb. I cry out as he begins to pull in and out of me at the same time, and I watch his face as he watches himself move inside my opening. The combination of his fingers on my clit and his cock inside me is quickly driving me crazy.

"Aaggh," I cry out intelligibly, and Nate's eyes snap up to my face. He removes his hand from my clit and leans forward so that both of his palms are spread on the comforter. My legs are still on his shoulders, and I can feel a good stretch in my hamstrings in this position. I'm also completely immobilized as he begins to drive into me in earnest now, his jaw tense and his neck muscles bulging.

I close my eyes and lose myself to the sensation of being drilled over and over again. He's hitting me so deeply, and I'm absolutely out of control and powerless. Maybe it would make me nervous with some other man, but I feel completely safe with Nate.

As an orgasm begins to rip through me, I feel his hands gripping my shoulders tightly, pulling me down against him as he comes inside me.

"Brynn, oh, fuck, Brynn!" he shouts as he releases himself. My legs fall off his shoulders and splay onto the comforter as he collapses on top of me. I gasp for air, and drowsily wipe the hair out of my face as I feel him stir on top of me. He picks his head up and listens for a moment. "They're still not home."

"Mm, guess not," I murmur rather incoherently.

"Good," he says with a wicked smile, and begins to kiss down the middle of my chest as he slides to his knees on the floor.

"Nate, what are you—oh, god," I moan, as he takes a long lick of my slit.

"I can't wait until tonight to taste you again. It's like I'm addicted to this, to you."

I close my eyes as he begins to flick his tongue across my clit. I thought I was completely worn out, but I'm coming back to life shockingly quickly under his deft tongue. His hands pin my knees to the sides of the bed, stretching me wide open so that he has complete access and control.

I feel his tongue dart in and out of me—a completely different sensation than when he uses his fingers. My back arches off the bed as he moves back to my clit, circling it relentlessly. I whimper as I feel waves of pleasure begin to reverberate through my body. My body wants to rock and shake, but Nate's hands pin me firmly to the bed, and his tongue keeps flicking across me. My energy has no choice but to be completely directed to the reaction he's eliciting. For some reason, it's when Nate backs off slightly that my body rocks into a full-out orgasm, my back arching wildly off the bed, just the top of my head and my hips remaining in contact with the comforter.

"Oh my god," I breathe as I relax down. I lift my head slightly and watch him lick his lips before lying down next to me on the bed and lazily flopping an arm over my waist.

"We should get dressed," he reminds me, kissing me quickly before jumping back up. I groan. Where's he getting all this energy? I feel like I could sleep for days.

"Do you think there will ever be a day when we can tell them?" I ask with a yawn as I sit up. He pauses for a moment as he pulls open a dresser drawer.

"I don't know. Let's just keep it our secret for now."

"No, no, I wasn't saying I—" I break off as we both hear a car pulling up to the front of the house. I hurry over to the pile of my clothes and ball them up in my arms before running to the door. "See you later!" I call quietly over my shoulder as I dash naked down the hallway.

As I shut my door behind me and begin pulling on my clothes, I wonder why Nate was so quick to suggest that we keep it quiet. Not that I want something different—for now, at least. But someday… I mean, does he just envision keeping our relationship secret forever? What kind of relationship would that be, anyway?

I sigh. These kind of questions are what Allison warned me about in the first place. It's just...*fuck*. What was once a far-off crush has become real for me. Too real. And Nate has said he has feelings for me, that I'm different, but he hasn't been any more specific than that.

On my end, I don't think this is a purely sexual infatuation. I'm really falling for him.

CHAPTER TWENTY-THREE

* * *

Going to work this week and being away from Nate during the day has felt like going through physical withdrawal. I really have to force myself to focus, because sometimes I find myself staring off into the distance, remembering what he did to me the previous night. I wish I could just go straight home at six today, but I promised Allison I'd go shopping with her. And there are actually a couple things I'd like to pick up for myself.

I meet her at the Anthropologie in Georgetown Mall, and we start going through the sale racks as we catch up. While she's not looking, I slip a couple sets of lingerie and sexy bras into my basket. I want to wear something a little sexy for Nate, but I don't want to face Allison's inevitable questions if she sees what I've picked out.

We eventually make our way to the changing rooms and begin trying on our choices. I quickly slip on the first matching set of bra and panties. I admire myself in the mirror. The lace is a pale violet, and not overtly sexy—it's Anthropologie, not Victoria's Secret, after all.

"What do you think?" Allison asks suddenly, pulling the curtain aside and stepping into the dressing room with me. She's wearing a blue cotton dress and twirls for a second before she realizes what I'm wearing. Her eyebrows raise. "Whoa."

"Allison," I groan, pulling one of the more substantial pieces of clothing off a hanger to cover myself.

"You know, I had a feeling something was different with you," she says, beginning to smile.

"Really?"

"Yup. And I was right. I always thought you two would make a good match."

"What? That's not what you said."

"Yeah, I totally called it!"

"No, you completely warned me against the whole thing," I reply, confused and even slightly annoyed.

"Wait," she says with a frown, "who are you talking about?"

"Who are *you* talking about?"

"Greg, obviously…"

"Oh, right."

"Brynn…"

"What?" I ask innocently.

"If it's not Greg, who did you think I was talking about?" she asks, her eyes widening.

"It's not important, OK?" I reply, blushing.

"Brynn, no. Please tell me it's not Nate. Please. I mean, he's your *stepbrother*. It's…it's *gross*."

"Thanks a lot, Allison. Not exactly what I needed to hear right now," I snap, turning my back to her to pull off the lingerie.

"Um, maybe it's *exactly* what you need to hear right now. I mean, what's with you? You're ignoring a perfectly nice guy to go out with some jock like Nate."

"Well, first of all, it's none of your business. Second of all, you're actually completely right about Greg. He is 'perfectly nice.' There's no spark at all.

Zero. Third of all, Nate's not 'some jock.' He's really smart, and kind, and funny. And with him? Sparks galore!"

"God, Brynn, I'm just trying to look out for you. You're making some really bad decisions."

I take a deep breath, not wanting to raise my voice in this public place. "No, Allison, you're not trying to look out for me. What you're doing is judging me. Completely different. And I really don't appreciate it." I finish pulling on my skirt and quickly slip my flats on as I grab my purse and walk quickly out of the dressing room.

I walk straight out of the store and toward the elevator to the parking garage, my cheeks burning with anger, though I also feel a bit like crying. I've never had a big fight like that with Allison before, and I don't like it.

I freeze outside another store just as I'm about to reach the elevators. Victoria's Secret. My relationship with Nate isn't "gross." There's nothing wrong with what we're doing. If anything, my conversation with Allison has made me want to lean into my relationship with Nate, not out of it. I march in and straight to the raciest pieces I see.

When I get home, I hear my mom and Pierce laughing in the kitchen, and the TV from the den. I walk in there and smile in relief at the sight of Nate with his feet up on the couch. He moves his legs over and I plop down.

"Hi," I murmur with a smile.

"Hi," he replies. "What's wrong?" I frown at him, and he reaches up to his shoulder, miming pulling at something. I stare at him for a moment before realizing he's mirroring my own action of pulling at my hair. I sigh and drop my hand.

"It's Allison. We had an argument," I explain. "She…she found out." He cocks his head and then lets out a low whistle as he realizes what I mean.

"Well, I suppose it's not that bad. I mean, I always thought…" he lowers his voice, looking back toward the kitchen where our parents are still talking. "I always thought that at school, we could be more open. No one really knows you're my stepsister there.

I mean, Allison would have found out then anyway, right?"

"I guess so…she just…she called it 'gross.' We're not, are we?"

"Well, I certainly don't think there's anything gross about you."

"It's more than that, though. I feel like we're drifting apart a little," I reveal, swallowing a ball of hurt in my throat.

"Mm," he replies, considering. "Like me and Jackson, sort of. Well, maybe you won't be quite as close as you were, but there are still things you can enjoy about her."

"When'd you get so wise?" I ask, nudging his feet next to me.

"Since I started hanging out with you. You're rubbing off on me."

Before I have time to consider whether he's being serious or not, we hear my mom call, "Dinner!" from the kitchen, and are forced to put our conversation on hold.

Pierce seems to be in an unusually good mood during the meal, for which I'm grateful. Not for his sake, but for Nate's, because he's much less likely to snap at his son when he's feeling jovial.

"Well, we haven't made an official announcement, Brynn, but Thornhill and Co. has just landed Mark Broadman as a client," he reveals eventually.

"The hedge fund billionaire?"

"That's right. He has several new holdings, and needs advice on some public policy matters."

"Wow, that's huge. Congrats, Dad," Nate chimes in. Pierce nods at him in a self-satisfied manner.

"I'm glad it's all—I'm glad that's happened, Pierce," I correct myself. I almost referenced the scandal earlier this summer, but managed to change course. We never talk about it now, though I know that Pierce was concerned that it would negatively impact his business. But landing such a big client is a good sign that people have moved on, and are on Pierce's side.

After dinner, Nate and I leave the dining room separately, while our parents remain there chatting. We always make a show of going our separate ways, to keep up appearances. I close my bedroom door knowing that he'll come for me around midnight, as he has every night this past week. My body quivers with excitement just thinking about it.

I consider writing an email to Allison, but decide I want a little more time to think about what to say. I turn to my purse and pull out the bag from Victoria's Secret that I stuffed to the bottom. I touch the black lace panties, a narrow diamond-shaped piece of fabric that just covers the essentials, with several thin strips, string, really, hooking around my hips and latching on to the back. The bra is conservative by contrast, though pretty with its Chantilly lace-covered cups.

I take a shower and then head downstairs for a cup of tea. I'm taking a mug down from the top cupboard when I feel Nate come up behind me. He wraps his hands around my waist and presses against me.

"Nate, not here!" I whisper.

"I know, I'm sorry," he murmurs in my ear. "I just want you all the time."

"I have a surprise for you tonight," I admit. He grinds his erection into my ass in response, his hands reaching under my shirt.

"You're killing me," he moans, then sighs, and rests his head on mine before pulling away. "See you soon." I lean against the counter as I hear him retreat, my skin tingling where he's touched it. I know that sneaking around won't work forever, but for now, there's something so hot about it.

I take my decaf Earl Grey up to my room, and change into the lingerie as I drink it, carefully pulling out the tags. I sink into bed with a yawn, pulling the sheet up over me. These late night assignations, while I wouldn't give them up for anything, are wreaking havoc on my sleep schedule.

The next thing I know, I'm being woken up by someone sinking into bed next to me. I turn into the warmth of Nate's body and slowly open my eyes.

"Sorry, should I just let you sleep?" he asks, kissing the top of my head.

"No way," I reply drowsily. "You have to have your surprise."

"Where is it?" he asks, looking around. I lift my arm and point down at my body. He grins, and pinches the top of the sheet in his fingers and begins to slowly pull it down. I bite my lip as I hear his sharp intake of breath as he reveals my bra. He pauses, looking up at my face.

"There's more," I promise him. He keeps pulling the sheet down, and finally pulls it over the barely-there panties. He tosses the sheet at my feet and runs his hand from my knee up my inner thigh.

"What shall I do with you tonight, Brynn?" he asks, eyeing my lingerie.

"Whatever you want," I breathe.

"Stand up," he says abruptly. I stand, and he eyes me up and down, licking his lips, then narrows his eyes. "You have any high shoes?"

"You mean heels?" I ask, with a smile. "Yeah."

"Put them on." I walk over to my closet and slip them on, then walk back.

"Better?" I ask, turning a little so he can see me from other angles.

"Nothing could make you look any better than you already do, Brynn. It wasn't about your appearance, it was about your height." I frown at him in confusion. "Come here," he says, walking over to the bedpost nearest to the door. I follow him. He takes me by the hips and moves me so that my back is pressed up against it. "You remember what happened in this exact spot? The first time I tried to kiss you, you denied me."

I smile. "I remember how much self-control it took."

"Good answer. Stay there." He walks over to my bureau and rummages around until he pulls out a couple of my old t-shirts and then walks back. "Close your eyes."

I obey, and feel him wrap one of the shirts around my head, tying it in the back but slightly to the side, so that it doesn't hit the bed post. As he steps back, I try to open my eyes to test the blindfold, and find I can't see anything.

"You trust me?" he asks. I nod. "Hands behind your back. Grip the bedpost." I feel my insides clench as I obey, spreading my palms against the solid wood of the bed. A moment later, I feel the other t-shirt wrapping around both my wrists and the posts, holding me securely against it. "Pull against it." I try, but don't get anywhere. "Good." I can sense him leaning in toward me, and feel the heat emanating from his body.

"Brynn, tonight I'm going to make you beg for it, understand?" I feel his warm breath against my cheek and squirm in anticipation against my bondage. "I'm going to deny you until you can't take it anymore. Until you beg me. Say that you understand."

"I understand." He's barely touched me, and I can already feel how wet I am against my new panties. Suddenly, I feel his fingertips on my arm, just above where the t-shirt is holding me to the bed. He trails his fingers lightly up my arm, barely touching me. My mouth drops open and I feel my heart rate speed up. His fingers continue across my clavicle, then down my other arm. As they make their way back up, I attempt to arch against him, but I can't.

He stops for a moment, then continues, his touch leaving a burning trail across my body. His fingers run straight down my chest and over the middle of my bra. Just as I think he's going to skip my breasts entirely, he moves back up and barely grazes the tops of my breasts, just above the cups. I gasp as he makes contact, but he quickly moves away, running his fingers down to my ribcage, then across my stomach. They dip for a moment into my belly button, and I hope he's going to continue down to my panties, but he skips them entirely, jumping down to the top of my thighs. He traces the length of one of my legs, then moves to the other.

As his fingers reach the top of my left leg, he breaks off contact. I feel sweat collect on my palms, despite the coolness of my bedroom. Where is he? Suddenly I feel his breath on my neck. Then his tongue is inside my ear, taking a long, languid lick. I moan, and my hands grip the bedpost more tightly. I hear him click his tongue.

"Brynn, we've barely even started."

I let my head fall back against the bedpost. How long is he going to torture me? As if in response, his hand slides up my neck to my chin, holding my face in place. His lips press against mine, roughly opening my mouth to his tongue. Then he steps into me, his legs spreading mine open, his arms wrapping tightly around my waist. The full contact is sweet relief, even if it does make me want him even more. His right hand glides over my ass and pulls me against his erection. My mouth is wide open to his, and our tongues massage each other's.

His other hand glides up my stomach and slips under my bra cup. I moan as I feel his calloused palm against my nipple. He pulls his mouth away quickly and leans his torso back. His fingers brush against the front of my bra for a moment, and then I feel his deft fingers unhook the front closure of my new bra. I feel my breasts spring out, and his thumbs brush against my nipples as he cups them in his hands. He begins to massage them more strongly, and suddenly I feel him sucking my right nipple into my mouth. He flicks his tongue across it as he sucks, then moves to my other side.

"I'm ready," I moan.

"Uh-uh, not yet," he replies, pulling my breast out of his mouth for a moment. Then he begins to trail kisses down my stomach, pausing for a moment to circle his tongue in my belly button. I feel him graze his fingers across the narrow strips of fabric on the sides of my panties. "I like these very much," he murmurs. "Maybe we'll try to keep these on."

Then he's gone. I hear the sounds of what could be his shirt being pulled over his head, but I can't be sure. There's silence for another minute, and I'm suspended in this pool of pleasure where he's left me, completely under his control.

I gasp as I feel him blow a stream of warm breath against my panties and feel my body shake involuntarily. His hands run up my thighs and then under the sides of my underwear, and I know he must be kneeling in front of me. I feel him slowly dip one finger under the right side of my panties, pulling them away from my body and tucking them to the other side. He blows on me again, and now his breath hits my clit directly.

"Spread your legs," he commands me quietly. I obey, inching myself out on my high heels. His tongue slides into my slit and I cry out.

"Oh, Nate," I moan, and he begins to flick his tongue back and forth across me. I unravel quickly, and he begins to speed up, circling his tongue rapidly. But just as I'm on the brink, my body arching as much as it can, he slows down again. I whimper. He doesn't stop completely, but he's not going fast enough to bring me release.

His right hand slips over my ass, under the fabric of my panties. I gasp as he slips one finger inside me. I've never had anything *back there.* He circles it inside me, mirroring his actions with his tongue. Once I get over my surprise at the foreign feeling, I find that I like it. On top of everything that he's already done to me, and is still doing, it's driving me right toward the edge again.

I moan as he slips two fingers from his other hand inside my opening, making a beckoning motion against my g-spot. I feel a spasm begin to rip through my body, but he pulls his mouth away completely. My knees almost buckle at the empty feeling he's left behind.

"Nate…" I protest. He leans back in, flicking his tongue once, hard, over my clit. My body ripples in response. The pleasure has built up inside me to such an extent that being unable to let go of it feels painful. I *need* him to let me come.

"Yes?" he answers innocently, and tortures me with another hard flick of his tongue, his fingers still circling slowly inside me.

"Please…" The pleasure is overloading my brain, and I can barely think.

"Please what?"

"I need you…please. I need you inside me right now. Please, I'm begging you. I'm begging you, Nate."

I almost faint with relief as he takes his fingers out of me and I hear the sound of a condom being ripped open. He steps into me and grabs one of my legs, wrapping it around his waist as he thrusts into me. I cry out at the contact. He drives in hard, slamming me against the bed post, and on just his second thrust, I feel my orgasm finally releasing through me as he presses into me again and again. His mouth covers mine as the last waves of pleasure crest over me. Even though I'm exhausted, I can feel that he's still hard inside me.

I feel him reach behind me, and realize that he's unknotting the t-shirt around my hands. My arms drop to my sides, and he pulls out of me. I feel him taking my hips and turning me, then he presses one hand roughly down on my back and I realize he's pressing my top half down onto the mattress. I turn my head to the side so I can breathe as he pulls my panties, still bunched to one side, to my ankles. His hand still holding me down, I feel him enter me from behind.

Even though I'm spent from my first orgasm and all the build-up leading to it, I feel my body begin to respond again. I feel him slide his thumb into my ass and gasp. I never realized how many nerves endings were back there.

"Brace yourself," he warns me, and begins to thrust harder into me. My fingers search for the edge of the bed and I'm just able to grasp it as he drives in deeper than he ever has before. He plunges into me again and again, hitting my g-spot directly every time. A second orgasm takes me by surprise, as though it was lying dormant until he awoke it. My body arches and shakes as I feel him pull out of me and a wetness cover my back. As my body quiets, I hear him hurrying to the bathroom and then him rubbing a tissue on my back.

"I'm sorry, I don't know why I did that," he murmurs.

"Hm? Did what?" I mumble, reaching up to remove the makeshift blindfold from my eyes.

"I…I came on you," he replies, halting his wiping motions to look me in the eye.

"Nate…it's OK. It doesn't bother me," I assure him.

"Really?" he asks, looking relieved. "I've never done that before, I just…I just wanted to see it on you, or something. I'm worried…I worry I push you too far."

"I like what we do together," I reply, stretching my arms above my head. "As far as I'm concerned, we're going to do a lot more, so you better get used to it."

"Is that so?" he asks, with a smile.

"Yep. Now clean me off. If we're going to do this again tomorrow night, I need to get some sleep."

CHAPTER TWENTY-FOUR

* * *

The next day, Thornhill and Co. is abuzz with the official announcement of Mark Broadman becoming a new client. There's talk that other high-profile investors could follow suit, including some of Broadman's contacts in Silicon Valley. Apparently the tech crowd is quite interested in influencing public policy. I'm just glad that everyone is in such a good mood, because it helps me fit in. My relationship with Nate, not to mention our late night sessions, has me practically glowing.

Constance talks to me happily in our cubicle, the awkwardness of our first day of working together having finally melted away over the summer months. She swivels in her chair and raises her eyebrows at me as Greg walks by, giving me a small wave.

"OK, what happened there?" she asks conspiratorially.

"It was nothing," I assure her, keeping my eyes on my computer, though I can see out of my periphery that she's still looking at me.

"Oh, come on. I won't tell. But it's obvious…I mean, for a couple weeks you guys were hanging out a bunch, and now he completely avoids you."

I sigh. "We went on a couple dates, and then we decided to break it off. But please keep it between us, alright?"

"Mmhm," Constance murmurs, swiveling back around. She can sense, rightfully so, that I'm not telling her the whole story.

Greg reacted as well as could be hoped when I told him I didn't want to go on any more dates with him. I blamed the office environment, and said I had extra pressure on me to be professional as the boss's stepdaughter, but I think he saw through that excuse. At least he could never guess the real reason. Now whenever I see him he's polite but standoffish.

I watch the corner of my screen, waiting to see if Allison will send me a Gchat message, but none arrives. I'll give it a little more time, and then reach out to her. I don't want to throw our whole friendship away over my relationship with Nate—not that we don't have some things to talk about. It's not that I need her approval exactly, but I do need her to stop judging.

"Lunch," Constance says, nudging me. I stand up and see other people making their way to the big conference room. Pierce has had lunch catered for the whole office to celebrate the new client. As we walk in, I notice that the temporary wall to the kitchen has been pulled back to make way for everyone. Pierce and Roderick, his business partner, stand by the buffet, happily talking with their employees. Pierce smiles at me as Constance and I make our way up to grab some plates.

"Roderick, you've met my stepdaughter Brynn, right?"

"Yes, good to see you again, Brynn," Roderick, a well-dressed man a bit younger than Pierce says, then turns away to shake someone's hand.

Pierce leans in. "You look particularly beautiful today, Brynn," he remarks.

"Oh, thank you, Pierce," I reply, a bit taken aback. Constance and I stand around the conference room for a while talking to the other interns, everyone sharing their plans for once they get back to school, and the rising seniors, like me, discussing what we'll do after we graduate. Eventually the crowd begins to thin out, and Constance and I each take a cupcake back to our cubicle.

"What's that? Vanilla?" she asks. I peer at the frosting.

"I think so, though I heard there were some coconut—" I break off as my desk phone rings. I look at it in surprise for a second—no one ever calls me on it—then reach forward to pick it up. "Brynn speaking."

"Brynn, it's Pierce. Could you come into my office for a moment?"

"Oh, sure, I'll be right there." I hang up and stand. "Pierce," I explain to Constance. "Probably wants to see if I'll be home for dinner tonight." She nods, and I walk down the hallway to his corner office. "He asked me to—" I explain to his secretary, Gwen.

"Sure, go on in," she replies, waving me in. I knock softly as I open the door. He beckons me inside and indicates I should take a seat across from his desk.

"Brynn, thanks for coming in," he says, standing and walking around his desk as he takes his reading glasses off and places them on his desktop calendar. I look at him curiously as he sits on the edge of his desk in front of me. "I know that I'm just your stepfather, but I hope that you know that you can always come to me with any…difficulties."

"Um, sure. Yes, thanks," I stumble, surprised by the direction of the conversation.

He stands and begins to pace behind my chair. "You're a very beautiful young woman, and I hope that you can see me as a sort of protector." I feel him come up and stand behind the chair. I start as he brushes my hair to the side and I feel his fingers graze against my skin just above the fabric of my dress. "I couldn't help but notice this," he says.

"What?" I ask, frowning.

"This bruise," he explains, still holding my hair to the side.

"Oh." My mind races. Shit. I bet I got it last night when Nate had me up against that bed post, and of course it's not in the sort of position where I'd see it. "Um, it's nothing. It's probably old, maybe from when I fell on that hike."

"I doubt it. I mean, how far does it extend…" I'm horrified to feel him unzip the top of my dress, all the way down to my bra strap. He spreads his fingers across my back and a sickening feeling spreads through my body with them. "Brynn, you have such a beautiful body. You shouldn't be with someone who treats you with less respect than you deserve." His fingertips just touch the top of my bra strap.

"Pierce!" I exclaim, and jump up. "I really don't think this is appropriate," I admonish him with as much confidence as I can muster, while reaching behind myself to pull my zipper up.

"Brynn, I'm just trying to look out for you. You clearly need a father figure in your life."

"I'm just fine, thank you very much," I reply shortly, glaring at him as I manage to zip my dress. I march to the door, taking a deep breath to compose myself as I walk through the door. I walk right past my desk and into the bathroom, quickly locking myself inside a stall. I lower the toilet seat and sit down, pressing my hands onto my burning cheeks. I know Pierce's words were saying one thing, but his actions, his touch, were saying quite another. It just felt wrong.

By the time I sit back down at my desk, I'm already second-guessing myself. Maybe I misread his behavior; maybe he was just trying to look out for me, but he's never had a daughter, so he didn't realize he was making me uncomfortable.

"You OK?" Constance asks over her shoulder.

"I'm fine," I reply, pushing my uneaten cupcake away. I'm not hungry anymore.

I manage to make it through the rest of the work day, though I know that I'll just have to see Pierce at home for dinner. As I drive home, I wonder if I should say I'm sick or something so I'll be able to just be by myself in my room. But as I walk in through the garage, my mom calls me into the kitchen. I carefully spread my hair over my neck to hide the bruises, then walk in.

"Oh, Brynn, honey, I'm so glad you're home. Come look," she gushes, pulling me into the dining room. I see that she's set it with fine china and crystal, and a massive vase of white lilies sits in the center. "I thought I'd do something a little special tonight to celebrate. What do you think?"

"Looks great, Mom," I reply half-heartedly. If she notices my downtrodden mood, she doesn't mention it, she just sweeps me back into the kitchen to show me the extravagant meal she's spent the day preparing.

When Pierce comes home about half an hour later, he quickly enters his study, calling to us that he has to make a quick call. My mom asks me to carry the roasted duck out on a silver tray, and I acquiesce, knowing I'd feel too guilty to fake sick when she's spent so much time on the food. When I walk back into the kitchen, Pierce is murmuring into my mom's ear as she blushes, so I quickly back out again.

I hear Nate enter through the front door, and he walks into the dining room just as I'm leaning on the back of my chair.

"Hey," he says with a smile. "I was thinking about you—" he breaks off as my mom and Pierce walk in. Pierce brandishes a bottle of champagne and walks around filling up our crystal flutes. I step back to give him a wide berth, and then we all sit down as he finishes filling up his own glass.

"Cheers," he says. I avoid his eye contact as we all clink our glasses. Nate frowns at me slightly and I know he can tell there's something up. Oh god, I can't even think about talking to him later tonight. He can always tell when I'm lying, so I don't know what I'm going to say.

"Brynn, did you messenger those envelopes like I asked?" Pierce says, turning to me.

"Hm?" I ask, startled by his question.

"The envelopes. I wanted to double check because you've seemed so distracted lately, and they're quite important."

I frown at him. What the hell? "You didn't ask me to messenger anything today, Pierce."

"Brynn," he sighs in a patronizing way, setting down his champagne glass.

"You didn't!" I reply, a little more defensively than I mean to. I glance at Nate and see him raising his eyebrows at me.

"You know that I did. And it's not like this is the first time this has happened," Pierce counters.

"Maybe we should—" my mom breaks in.

"Wait, no," I say to her, holding up my hand. "I honestly don't know what you're talking about Pierce."

"Well, this clearly isn't the time to discuss it, but since you're pressing me, I've heard from some of your immediate superiors that you haven't been very responsible."

"What? Like who? When?"

"Obviously I can't give you exact dates, and I need to protect their anonymity—"

"Wow. Wow," I snap, tossing down my napkin. "You are just making all this up, aren't you?"

"Brynn, calm down," Nate murmurs from across the table.

"Calm down? Seriously? He's lying!"

"He has no reason to—" Nate argues.

"He damn well does. He called me into his office today and unzipped my dress, and I told him to back off, and now he's pissed."

"You know that's because I was worried about those bruises on your neck, Brynn. Don't get hysterical."

"You're a liar," I whisper.

He slams his hand down on the table, causing me to jump. "I will not be spoken to that way in my own house!"

I glance back and forth at my mom and Nate, speechless. Are they really just going to sit there staring at me? I stand up so abruptly that my chair almost falls over backward. I can't take being surrounded by this bullshit anymore. I walk quickly around the table and then out the front door, clenching my fists to try to contain my anger until I'm outside.

As I close the door behind me, I pick up my pace, walking straight down the driveway and out of the gates. The woods rise up quiet and dark around me as tears of frustration and humiliation begin to stream down my face. I don't know where I'm going—I just need to get away from that house.

"Hey! Wait!" I hear a woman's voice call out behind me, but I keep walking. "You're Brynn, right?"

I freeze and take a deep breath before turning around. "Look, if you're a reporter or something, I'm really not in the mood." I can just see her blonde hair reflect the moonlight as she takes a couple steps closer.

"I'm not a reporter. I'm Nate's mom, Eileen."

CHAPTER TWENTY-FIVE

* * *

"Are…are you alright?" she asks, taking another step toward me.

"I'm, I'm just—" I break off as a sob escapes my lips. "I'm sorry."

"It's alright. I've got some tissues in my car— why don't you come sit down for a moment."

I nod. In a saner moment, I might have questioned the safety of getting into a strange woman's car, but this is not a sane moment. She wraps her arm around my shoulders and leads me to the passenger side of her blue sedan, parked just down the street from the gates of the house. She sits me down then hurries around to the driver's side and gets in.

"Here you go," she says, pulling a box of tissues from the floor of the back seat.

"Thanks," I murmur rather incoherently. She flips on the car's overhead light. "Oh!" I exclaim. "You're the woman from the boathouse parking lot."

She smiles wryly. "I thought you saw me that day. I'm not a stalker or anything. It's just, sometimes I like to get a glimpse of him, that's all. See what he looks like, how he's doing."

"I understand."

"But what's happened to you? Is there anything I can do?"

"It's Pierce," I murmur as more tears fall from my eyes at the mention of his name.

"What'd he do now?"

"He…he made a pass at me at work. I mean, I actually wasn't sure that's what it was right after, but then tonight he got on my case about something I didn't even do, and that's when I knew for sure."

"Oh, sweetie, I'm sorry," she says, rubbing my shoulder. "Pierce has a serious case of entitlement. He thinks that anything with a vagina is fair game, even his stepdaughter, it seems."

"I mean, I already knew he was an asshole from the way he treats Nate, but I just hadn't felt it directed at me yet."

She stills. "He doesn't treat Nate well?" she asks quietly.

"Oh, oh, I'm sorry," I reply, looking at her through bleary eyes. "He's…he's very hard on Nate. He calls him entitled, selfish, when I think those are really things he knows deep down are true about himself."

"My little Nate," she murmurs to herself.

"But he's really…Nate is a good person, you should know that. Well, to be honest, at first I thought he was more like Pierce, but that's just a cover. Maybe it's that half his genes are yours, or maybe his father raised him to be a better person than he is himself, I don't know. But he's smart, funny, hardworking…"

"Thank you," she says, taking my hand. "I'm sorry you have to go through this. Did you tell your mom?"

"She found out at dinner, but…" I shake my head. "She's completely under Pierce's spell. She gets like that about men, but I've never seen her quite so enamored of one before him. She looks a lot like you, actually," I realize, studying her beautiful, slightly lined face.

"Pierce certainly has a type," she says with a sad smile.

"There's another thing you should know…about Nate…I found out after you called: he thinks you left because he was too much for you, because he was a bad kid, basically. I tried to talk to him about it, really, but he wouldn't hear it."

"Nate was a wonderful child, and even if he'd been the devil incarnate, I still wouldn't have left him."

"Yeah, I figured as much. He said that the night before you left, you and Pierce had a big fight over him, because he misbehaved, and that's why you left the next day."

"Oh, god," she murmurs, covering her face in her hands. "He must have felt so alone, so responsible.

No…I remember that fight, because it was our last. We'd been to some big gala that night, and we'd seen this woman there who was in our circle at the time. I knew he'd cheated before, but he promised me he'd stopped, and then at this party, I could just tell by the way they looked at each other that they were sleeping together. I confronted him about it at home, and he barely even bothered to deny it. I was yelling at him, asking what kind of example he was setting for his son. I left…I never thought that would be one of the last times I'd see Nate. I never thought that was even a possibility."

"I want to help you," I say suddenly.

"What? No. You have too much going on already," Eileen says, shaking her head emphatically.

"No, I want to. Not just for you, either. For Nate. He needs you in his life. I can tell that you're good, and kind, and he needs people like that to love him. Please let me help you."

"I don't want to put you in a position…I don't want to jeopardize anything. You and Nate, you have a special relationship."

"Um, sure, yeah, he's a great guy," I hedge.

"Brynn…it's OK. I know."

I swallow. "Know what?"

"When I saw you that day at the boathouse, I could just tell. At first I thought you were his girlfriend, and then I realized who you were, and I saw the way you two looked at each other. You're in love," she whispers. I begin to tug at my hair nervously. Shit. Shit. "You've acted on your feelings?" It's all I can do to nod. "Do your parents know?" I shake my head. "Brynn, you don't have to be embarrassed. Life's messy. People find love wherever they can. Hell, it's not like you're breaking any laws."

My tears begin to slip down my face again, renewed. "I can't believe it's so obvious."

"Maybe I just caught you two in an unguarded moment. But, see, if Nate and you are together, I don't want to come between you."

"Honestly, I'd like him to meet you. I think it might do him some good. When Pierce was chewing me out tonight, he didn't say anything."

"I'm sorry."

"So you'll meet with him?"

"If you're sure it's OK with you."

"I'm not sure how I'll set it up yet, but write down your number for me, and I'll get in touch with you when I know."

She nods and tears a slip of paper from a paperback book in the back seat. As she hands it to me and I get out of the car, she leans over into the passenger seat.

"Brynn, if I could just give you a little advice…I would avoid Pierce for the next few days. He doesn't like it when people stand up to him."

I nod and shut the door, walking slowly back to the house as I run my fingers over her phone number. I peer cautiously through the first floor windows, not wanting to walk back in on dinner, but it looks like they've finished and the plates have all been cleared. I quietly open the front door and tiptoe up the stairs to my bedroom, locking my door behind me. I put Eileen's phone number on my bureau and am just about to change out of my dress when I hear a soft knock on the door. Usually Nate just comes in now, so he clearly knows that I'm upset with him. I walk over and unlock it, then open it a few inches.

"You locked it?" he asks, looking hurt.

"I want to be alone right now," I murmur, though a knot forms in my throat at the thought of spending the first night in a week without him.

"I…I can't choose between you," he whispers. He looks so forlorn, and I see a glimpse of the little boy that he once was, overhearing his parents' arguments.

"I know."

"They're going to some charity lunch tomorrow afternoon…maybe we could spend some time together."

"OK," I nod, my mind already moving in a different direction.

He pauses, unsure if he should kiss me. "Alright, goodnight," he says, and walks down the hallway to his bedroom.

I close and lock the door after him, then grab my cell phone and put in Eileen's number. *Tomorrow afternoon,* I text her. *I'll let you know when my parents are gone, and then you come meet Nate.*

CHAPTER TWENTY-SIX

* * *

I yawn as I sit by my window, waiting for the sounds of my mom and Pierce leaving. I wasn't able to sleep well at all last night. There were too many worries rattling around in my brain. Mainly, though, it felt strange not to see Nate. I missed his presence in my bed with a physical ache that gnawed away at me.

Finally I hear some movement in the rest of the house. I walk to my door and crack it open, sticking my head out into the hall. I can just hear my mom murmuring something to Pierce as they make their way to the garage. Soon I hear the car pulling out of the driveway and I glance at the clock. I'll give them ten minutes.

I wait impatiently, and as soon as it's up, I text Eileen and head down to the foyer. Luckily Nate has been safely ensconced in his room all morning. I don't know if he even got up to train this morning, which is highly unusual for him. I glance out the window next to the door and see Eileen walking up the driveway.

"Hi," I murmur quietly as she reaches the steps and I open the door.

"Hi," she replies nervously, smoothing her blouse. "Do I look alright?"

"You look fine," I assure her. I can't imagine how she must feel, finally seeing her son face-to-face after all these years. She looks around the foyer.

"God, this place is even bigger than it looks from outside."

"I know. It's ridiculous," I agree, and usher her into the den. "Pierce and my mom are at some charity lunch, so they'll be gone for a while," I tell her. She bites her lip nervously and takes a seat on the couch. "I'll call Nate down, alright? I haven't told him anything…I wasn't sure he would come otherwise." She nods, and I head to the stairs. "Hey, Nate?" I yell, and hear his bedroom door open. "You wanna come down to the den?"

I feel a fissure of guilt as he replies happily, "Sure! Be right there," and I hear him moving around.

I don't like the idea of setting a trap and lying to him, but I rationalize that it's in the service of a greater truth, that of the true nature of his parents' relationship, and his father's character.

I walk back into the den, and stand nervously next to the couch where Eileen's sitting. She stands as we hear Nate walking down the stairs, and then he turns the corner and sees us. His face is a blank as he surveys the scene before him. He takes a step forward, looks like he's going to say something, and then steps back.

"Nate, it's me, your mom," Eileen whispers.

"I know who you are," Nate replies quietly. He turns to me. "You did this?"

"I think you should hear what she has to say. Please, will you just sit for a minute?"

Nate's face twists into a sneer—an expression I haven't seen in weeks. "You're unbelievable," he spits at me, and storms out the front door, slamming it behind him. Eileen sits down with a muted cry, and I run after him.

"Nate!" I call as I shut the door behind me and head down the front steps. He's walking around the side of the house, probably headed for the garage and his car to make an escape. "Would you just listen to me for a second?"

"Why? So you can try to poison my mind against my dad some more?" he yells, reeling around.

"I'm trying to tell you the *truth* about him! Eileen can tell you—"

"Oh, so this is all about *you*! You can try to paint it as some benevolent way of getting a mother and son to reunite, but really, this is all about getting me to believe your story," he turns again and begins to walk away across the grass.

"No! That's not true!" I protest, pursuing him. "Your mom is a good person—I wanted to help her, and you."

"You're pathetic, you know that?" he says, spinning around again. "Stop following me. Whatever mistakes we made together this summer, it's over."

"What? Nate, I—" I feel like he just punched me in the gut. How did this all go so wrong?

"I thought maybe you were different than all the other girls I've fucked, but you're not, OK? From now on, let's just smile at each other politely from across the room at family events, like *normal* stepsiblings do."

"No, no! We *are* different, we are."

"You're just attached because I was your first. Don't worry about it, you'll get over it soon. You were nothing special to me, Brynn," he says and walks through the garage's side door. I stand in shock as I watch the garage door slide open and his Wrangler come speeding out. I watch him head down the driveway, then disappear around the corner.

I hear the front door open behind me, and Eileen approach me. "I'm so sorry, Brynn, this is all my fault."

"No, it's not," I reply, biting my lip to keep from sobbing.

She puts her arm around me. "He's just angry. He'll come to his senses."

"No, he's just as stubborn as I am. It's really over." I collapse against her, burying my head on her shoulder as I begin to cry.

"First love always hits the hardest," she murmurs as she rubs my arm. "Come on—your parents won't be back for a while. I'll make you some tea."

* * *

After Eileen leaves and I've hidden away in my room, I can't help but marvel at her kindness. It's been a long time since my own mother has taken care of me and comforted me the way she did, even though the afternoon might have gone even worse for her than it did for me. She told me that she's learned not to get her hopes up for a reunion over the years, though it does still hurt.

I keep picturing the anger on Nate's face as he ended our romantic relationship. I could tell he really meant the things he was saying. My body aches at the thought that I won't get to touch him again, and feel him against me. Already I feel like it's been ages since I've seen him.

I hear my mom and Pierce come home in the late afternoon, and I glance at my locked door. I don't want to see them now, or anytime soon, for that matter. I think of how Nate begins to resemble his father when he gets angry, but his mother in his kindness. Even though she was only in his life until he was eight or nine, she must have had some influence on him in those early years, in addition to whatever good traits she passed down to him genetically. I suppose I wanted to tip the scales in her direction, to make sure that Nate keeps listening to the side of himself that his mother has passed on to him. But clearly, I don't have the power to make such a thing happen.

Mistake. He referred to what happened between us as a mistake. My body curls around myself as though I've just been punched in the gut. I can feel the pain reverberating in my bones. *I thought maybe you were different than all the other girls I've fucked, but you're not. You're nothing special to me, Brynn.* His words keep echoing around in my head, and I can't make them go away. I don't know if I've ever felt so completely hollow before.

Eventually, I fall asleep, my body finally giving in to the exhaustion I feel. When I wake up, it's almost ten at night. My mom didn't even try to wake me for dinner, I realize. I feel a surge of anger against her. Mothers are supposed to protect their children, but of course she's taking Pierce's side. She thinks he's some kind of savior, rescuing her and her abandoned daughter from some lonely life. I want to scream. I want her to be stronger, to be there for me like I've been there for her countless times. But I know my anger is useless; I've long ago realized that I can't change her, can't expect her to be any different from the way that she is.

My stomach grumbles, reminding me that I've skipped a meal or two today. I don't even feel like eating, but I know that I'll never be able to get to sleep again tonight without a little something in my stomach. I sigh and get out of bed and head over to my bureau, pulling a sweatshirt on over my t-shirt. I cautiously open my door and listen. I think I can just hear the sounds of the TV from my mom and Pierce's room. Should be safe, then. I tiptoe down the hallway, pausing at the open door to Nate's dark room. Still out, I guess. Probably drinking somewhere.

How long can this situation last? I wonder as I walk quietly down the stairs. I feel like we're all tightly-wound strings, and one of us is bound to break sometime. I know I for one can't keep creeping around the house like this, avoiding everyone.

In the kitchen, I fix myself a grilled cheese sandwich, feeling the need for some comfort food. I'm just turning off the stove top when I hear the door to Pierce's study open. I hurry to grab the spatula and slide the sandwich onto my plate before he comes in, but I'm too late.

"Brynn," he says from the doorway. "We missed you at dinner."

Ugh, that asshole, acting like nothing happened. "Just fixing something now," I answer shortly. As I put the spatula and pan into the sink, I see over my shoulder that he's walking toward me. He plants himself between the island and the fridge, trapping me by the counter.

"Your mother is very upset," he tells me, his eyebrow bending into a concerned frown.

"Is she?" I ask through gritted teeth. If he expects me to apologize, as though her mood is my fault, then he's mistaken.

"Brynn, I think you've gotten the wrong idea about me," he murmurs, taking another step toward me. I reluctantly turn to face him. "You have no idea how hard it is for a man, to have a beautiful woman like you in the house."

"I'm your stepdaughter, Pierce," I practically growl as my heartbeat jumps in my chest.

"You've really blossomed this summer, Brynn. You've become a woman," he says, stepping into me. I can feel his warm breath on my face.

"I want you to get away from me," I whisper, my throat tightening.

"Just for a moment…I need to feel…" he moans pitifully, sliding his hand onto my hip and then over my ass. My anger ignites at his touch, blasting away my fear. I get my arms up between us and shove him away.

"Get off me, you fucking asshole!" I scream. He looks at me in shock. "You think you're some gentleman with your fancy suits and your mansion, but inside you're just some sick pervert, taking advantage of anyone you can. I see who you really are, even if no one else does."

His face twists with anger, and I feel my cheek light up with pain before my brain can process that he's slapped me. I bring my hand up to my burning face, my head still pulled to the side, just as Pierce disappears in a blur.

I straighten up with a gasp as I realize Nate has just tackled him to the floor, and they are now grappling fiercely on the kitchen tiles.

"Don't you fucking touch her!" he yells at his father, whose face is turning red in an effort to defend himself against his much stronger son. I hear footsteps from the stairwell and see my mom running down the hallway and manage to unfreeze myself.

"Nate! Nate, stop!" I yell, as he manages to find the top position. My mom screams as Nate punches Pierce hard across his jaw. I throw myself on Nate's back as he cocks his arm back in preparation for another punch. "Nate, I'm OK, I'm OK," I repeat in his ear. I feel him relax a little and begin to pull him up. He drops his arm and stands up with me. Pierce pushes him away as he stands up, too, and they face off, each breathing heavily, Pierce with a trail of blood dripping from the corner of his mouth.

"What's going on?" my mom finally whispers, her voice full of fear.

"I saw everything," Nate growls, addressing his father. "You hypocrite."

To my shock, Pierce begins to laugh. "I knew it, I knew it! Look at you two!" he says, pointing at us.

"What's he talking about?" my mom asks, glancing at me.

"They're fucking!" Pierce bursts out.

"No…what?" my mom murmurs.

"Oh, Christ, Holly, are you really that fucking stupid? You didn't even suspect?"

My mom shakes her head. "That's why you're fighting?"

"No," Nate says, turning to her. "I saw him trying to feel up Brynn, and then she told him to stop, and he slapped her."

A look of horror spreads across my mom's face. She looks at me, then at Pierce.

"Is this true? *Is it true?*" Pierce doesn't even bother responding to her accusations, just turns his palms upward and shrugs. A wailing cry escapes my mom's lips. For a second I think she's going to collapse, but then she throws herself at Pierce, her limbs a blur as she attacks him. "I trusted you! I trusted you!" she screams. Pierce puts his arms up to defend himself as Nate steps forward and wraps his arms around her, hemming her in and then pulling her away. "My own daughter! My own daughter, you son of a bitch!"

With a strangled cry, she turns her head and begins to sob against Nate's chest. Pierce surveys the three of us, aligned against him on the other side of the kitchen.

"Nothing?" Nate whispers, as he rubs my mom's shoulder. "You have nothing to say for yourself?"

"Come on, Nate. You're really going to believe them?" Pierce says, a sneer of contempt on his face.

"I don't have to—I saw you with my own eyes. But I should have believed Brynn in the first place," Nate says quietly, though I can hear the strength in his voice. Pierce can only manage a snort of derision before he walks toward the hallway. "My mother," Nate says, and Pierce stops, his back still toward his son. "You made everything up, didn't you?"

Pierce stands frozen for a moment, his head slightly cocked to the side. I can't see his face, and can't imagine what could be going on inside his mind. His carefully crafted history, now falling apart around him. He shakes his head slightly, as if waving away an unpleasant smell, then continues to walk down the hallway. He heads straight to the front door, and shuts it behind him. As we hear the sound of his car heading down the driveway, my mom straightens up, and Nate's arms fall to his sides.

"I need to be alone for a little while," she murmurs, her gaze on the floor, and walks unsteadily toward the stairs. I watch her leave, wishing she had the strength to comfort me for even a moment.

"She's just in shock," Nate says, reading my mind like always.

"I know," I reply with a nod, struggling to keep myself together.

"I should have believed you."

"I had no reason to lie."

"I know. I just couldn't believe he was capable of that kind of thing, or maybe I didn't *want* to believe."

"You said some awful things to me today. God, was that just today?" I ask with a sad laugh, reaching up to rub my forehead.

"I'm so sorry, Brynn. I was angry…sometimes my temper…I didn't mean any of those things. The time we've spent together—" he says, taking a step toward me.

"No, no. I'm not ready for that. I don't know if we can go back…" I murmur, a tear slipping down my face.

"Brynn, please, I can't lose you."

"You were so ready to turn on me," I whisper. "So ready to push me away and be done with me."

"I was in shock at seeing her again. I didn't actually mean it."

"But you *said* it, didn't you? The way I care about you…I would never treat you that way, would never want you to hurt. But you wanted me to hurt. You don't feel the way about me that I feel about you. You can't."

"That's not true! You have no idea how much I care about—"

"I love you." There's a long silence. I stare up into his beautiful face, my heart shattering as he doesn't reply. He just looks back down at me, some unknowable emotion flickering across his eyes. "Well, there you go. There you go. Goodbye, Nate," I say, turning my back to him. He doesn't move.

"What are you going to do?" he finally asks quietly.

"Um, well," I begin with a cold laugh. "I think I'm going to eat this cold grilled cheese sandwich, and then I'm going to start packing."

CHAPTER TWENTY-SEVEN

I survey my mom's old beat-up station wagon. Both the car and our old house were just on the verge of being sold, but my mom was able to back out. Luckily she was taking her time in the process because she didn't think she had to worry about money anymore. The car isn't even full—the only things that belonged to us here were our clothes and some knick-knacks. It only took me a few hours this morning to pack it up. It's both sad and comforting. Our old life is still waiting for us, almost as though this whole summer never happened.

But of course it did. I wondered last night if I would take these last few months back if I could. If I were given a magic wand that could make it so that my mom had never met Pierce, that I'd returned to our old house for the summer, that my relationship with Nate had never gone beyond that encounter in the crew house, would I wave it?

I don't know if I've ever felt so much pain as I have recently, but also never so much happiness. I was held in such a tight little shell before, never really experiencing the depths or heights of anything, and I suppose you can't have one without the other.

To never have held Nate in my arms...no, I can't imagine it. Despite so many terrible things having happened, I would never want to erase the time I spent with him, even if it would take away the pain I'm feeling right now. The pain that I can feel even in my bones, causing a throbbing ache throughout my whole body. It's like I'm detoxing from some powerful, addictive substance. One that I know only hurts me in the end.

I catch a glimpse of my slightly swollen lip in the car window from where Pierce hit me last night. We haven't seen him today—he must be holed up at a friend's house or a hotel. I don't even want to think of the divorce proceedings that my mom will be wrapped up in now.

I hear the front door shut behind me and turn—will it be Nate coming to say goodbye? But it's my mom, carrying one last small suitcase, her eyes covered in large, round sunglasses.

"Ready?" she asks, without looking at me. I nod, then remember one last thing I've forgotten.

"I'll be right back," I say, and hurry in through the front door without explanation. I walk straight up the staircase and down the hall into my bedroom. It looks exactly the same as the first time I saw it. I pause for a moment, taking in the beauty of the furnishings for the last time, before walking over to my desk and opening the top drawer. I reach my arm all the way to the back and fish out the small slip of paper I stashed there.

I walk out and down the hallway. Nate's bedroom door is slightly open and I can tell from the silence that he's not inside. I push it open all the way and walk to his bed. I run my hand over his bedspread and breathe in his smell. I pull down the comforter and lay the piece of paper on top of his pillow, then pull the comforter back up over it. I certainly don't want Pierce to find the scrap of paper where Eileen wrote her phone number.

I'm about to leave when something makes me cross over to his window overlooking the river. My eye catches on a flash of white on the lower lawn: Nate sitting on the top step of the stairs leading down to the rocky shore. He sits completely still, his white t-shirt stretched across his broad back. I resist the urge to wonder what he'll do now—it's really none of my business anymore.

I hurry back down to the car and see my mom sitting in the passenger seat. I open the driver's door and see that she's placed the keys on the seat. I get in without a word and turn the car on then pull away from the house. I glance in the rearview mirror to get one last glimpse at it as I turn the corner out of the gate.

My mom is silent on our drive back to our old house, just staring out the window as we get on the highway that takes us further away from the city, back to our much less expensive neighborhood. A seed of resentment that's been building inside of me all summer, or perhaps longer, finally takes root as I glance sidelong at her impassive face.

"You haven't even looked at me all day," I finally say, gripping the steering wheel with white-knuckled hands.

"What do you mean?" she asks faintly, still not turning to me.

"You haven't looked at my face," I repeat.

"Brynn…" she sighs.

"No, it's true. Your husband *slapped* me last night and you never even came to check on me. And now you won't look at the bruise."

"Brynn, I've been very upset."

"And I haven't? He feels me up, hits me, and you haven't asked me if I'm OK."

"It's not my fault that he did those things!" she shouts, suddenly hysterical.

"Mom, I'm not blaming you for his actions, alright? But you're my mother. You should have believed me—you should have taken care of me. I've been taking care of you for years, and this time, *I* needed *you*."

My mom sobs once, reaching up to cover her mouth with her hand. "I wanted to believe you,

Brynn, I really did," she finally gasps. "I just knew that if I did, everything would fall apart, and it all seemed so perfect."

"But it wasn't."

"No, it wasn't." I feel her hand reach up tentatively to touch my face, and her fingers graze over the small cut in the corner of my mouth. "Oh, I'm so sorry, my darling. Does it hurt much?"

"Hardly at all," I reply, swallowing the tears that have sprung up at her touch.

"I never guessed…about you and Nate, I mean," she whispers.

"That's over, too," I reply shortly as my emotions threaten to overwhelm me.

"Ah," is all she says. "Well, I know that might not be the kind of thing you ever want to talk about with your mother, but I'm here. You cared about him a lot?"

"Yes," I answer, my voice raspy with held emotion. "So I guess you have to get a lawyer?" I ask, changing the subject.

"Oh, god. I suppose so," she replies. "I think I'll be able to get my old job at the salon back, at least. I talked to Anita and she said the new girl they got is terrible."

"Did you sign a pre-nup?" I ask, thinking of Eileen. I know I'll have to fill my mom in on what I know about her soon, but it would just be too much for me right now.

"Yes," she sighs. "Iron-clad."

CHAPTER TWENTY-EIGHT

* * *

I close the door behind me and dump my newly-purchased textbooks on my thin mattress, then straighten up to survey my Lawn Room. It's not much to look at, with its sparse furnishings and lack of bathroom access, though it does have a framed list of every inhabitant that's lived here, going back to UVA's very first class.

For the last month, I've just been sitting around our old house, doing my best to help my mom with getting her old job back and hiring a lawyer, but there really wasn't much for me to do. I felt both relief and fear when it was finally time to drive back down to Charlottesville. Relief because I'll have schoolwork to occupy my mind, and fear because I might run into Nate on campus.

Foolishly, I had hoped that he would try to get in touch with me after my mom and I moved out, but he didn't. It really was stupid of me. I told him that I loved him, and he didn't say it back. Simple as that. Even though he was angry, there must have been some truth to his words when he told me I wasn't special to him.

I glance at the clock. Just after four—almost time for my dinner shift in the cafeteria to be starting. I change into my work clothes and head over. At least I know I won't run into Nate there—the athletes all have a separate dining hall serving far tastier and more nutritious food. I open my door to the lawn, smiling halfheartedly at another female student a few doors down as she exits her room at the same time. I walk quickly, keeping my head down, not really wanting to interact with anyone I know. I enter the dining hall and cross around to the side door, back into the kitchen.

"Oh, Brynn!" Roberta, my manager, waves to me from a table by the front, where she's doing some paperwork. I wave back and head over. "There's been some issue with your work-study," she tells me quietly as I reach her.

"An issue?" I ask frowning. "Do you know what it is?"

"Something related to your scholarship—that's all the dean's office told me when they called." I rub my forehead in frustration. This is the last thing I need. "If you head over to Monroe Hall now, you might be able to talk to someone who knows more than I do." I nod. "Sorry," she adds, before continuing with her work.

I hurry out of the dining hall and follow Roberta's advice to see if I can get some more answers, though I fear I already know what happened. My mom has been so frazzled lately, I bet she forgot to make a payment on the portion of the tuition that we still owe. I explain the situation to a secretary at Monroe, who points me toward the office in charge of the work-study program. A man in his early thirties stands to greet me as I walk through the open door of his office.

"Francis Delton," he introduces himself, shaking my hand. "How can I help you?"

"Well, I was told there's some issue with my work-study program, or with my scholarship, or something," I reply, reaching to tug at my hair before realizing it's pulled up in a ponytail.

"OK, your name?" he asks, sitting down and motioning me into the chair across from him.

"Brynn Atwell," I respond, spelling it out for him. He types my name into his computer and then clicks around for a moment.

"Ah, this is quite unusual," he says, raising his eyebrows at his screen.

"OK…" I reply nervously.

"You can no longer participate in the work-study program, because your tuition has been paid in full."

I stare at him. "You mean, for this semester?"

"No, I mean all of your tuition."

I shake my head, unable to believe him. "For this year? Or…I mean, not *all* all?"

He smiles. "*All* all."

"But that's…that's impossible. How? Who?" I stammer.

"I have no idea. I can only see that you're ineligible for the program."

"OK, OK," I reply, trying to gather my thoughts. "Thank you. Thank you so much." I wander out of his office and out onto the quad. With Pierce and my mom getting divorced, I knew I'd have college tuition loans to deal with again, and I took it in stride. I was used to the idea, anyway. What the hell's going on?

I reach into my back pocket and dial my mom. I have no idea if she'll know either, but I can at least tell her the good news.

"Oh, Brynn! Brynn, I was just going to call you!" she says as she picks up.

"Let me guess, is it about my tuition?" I ask, hearing excitement in her voice.

"Yes! How did you know?"

"Well, I showed up for my shift at the dining hall, and was told that my tuition's been taken care of. What's going on?"

"I was literally just picking up the phone to tell you…it all happened so quickly this afternoon. Pierce's lawyer offered me a settlement in the divorce! And it specifically included payment of your tuition."

"Pierce paid my tuition?" I ask, my mind reeling.

"Yes! As soon as I signed, the money was wired over."

"But…but mom, was it a good settlement? I mean, did you have a lawyer look it over?"

"Yeah, it was the same lawyer who told me I'd get nothing because of the pre-nup I signed. He was completely floored, and told me I'd better sign before Pierce changes his mind."

"But…why? I mean, it seems so out of character for him."

"I know! I can hardly believe it either. It's crazy! I'll be able to pay off the mortgage on the house and have a little left over. I mean, we're not rich or anything, but we have a bit of leeway now."

"Was it, you know, 'hush money,' do you think?"

"I doubt it. The lawyer said that there's no less reliable witness than a woman trying to defame her ex-husband, so I don't really think Pierce would be worried about me going to the press with stories or anything—not that I'd want to do that anyway. But honey, it's done now. It's really over. We don't have to worry about him anymore."

"Well, I'm glad that you're happy with it. If you're happy I'm happy. Man, this is the first good news we've gotten in a while, huh?" I touch my lips with my fingertips, wondering when the last time I smiled was.

"Have you seen him yet?" my mom asks quietly. She doesn't need to specify that she's referring to Nate.

"Not yet," I reply. "Though I've convinced myself that every brown-haired guy I've seen from the back is him."

"That's normal," my mom assures me. "You'll see him everywhere for a while. But it will pass soon, my darling. I promise."

CHAPTER TWENTY-NINE

* * *

Realizing I now have the evening off, I take a deep breath and call Allison. I'm still in a daze, but I want to share my good fortune with her and Miriam. Allison and I haven't talked since our argument over the summer, so I'm relieved when she accepts my invitation on behalf of both of them. I pick a rather fancy restaurant, and assure her that it's my treat.

Half an hour later, I'm walking out of my room in a light summer dress—the weather here in Virginia is still sweltering, even though it's September. I walk slowly across the quad to the off-campus restaurant, trying not to work up a sweat. I watch a group of freshmen girls giggling as they head out for a group dinner. New hall mates, no doubt. I remember how nervous I was my first year here, worrying that I wouldn't make any more friends than I did in high school.

My insides contract as I pass the spot where I first saw Nate crossing the grass, just a couple weeks into my freshman year. I shake my head at myself. I have to forget him.

When I reach the restaurant, an upscale Mexican place known for its flavored margaritas, I'm relieved to feel the AC hit me. The hostess smiles at me just as I see Allison sitting in a booth by herself. She stands with a nervous smile and I walk over.

"I hope you don't mind," she murmurs as we hug awkwardly. "I sort of lied to Miriam and told her you pushed back dinner by fifteen minutes so we'd have a chance to talk."

A short bark of laughter escapes my mouth. "I don't know if I've ever heard you lie before." To my surprise, she blushes as we sit down across from each other.

"Well, I've been thinking about what you said…about my being judgmental…and maybe I am a bit of, you know, a goody two-shoes. Maybe I need to loosen up a little. What I'm trying to say is, I'm sorry for what I said."

I reach over and place my hand over hers. "Thanks. It means a lot to hear you say that. I've hated not talking to you."

"Me too," she replies. I see her glance over my shoulder.

"And here I thought I was early!" I hear Miriam say. I stand up to give her a hug. "I see you two have synced your watches, being in the same city together all summer! Ugh, I was so jealous!" She sits down with a dramatic sigh in the booth next to Allison, her bright red hair falling onto her shoulder. "So. Catch me up on everything that's been happening."

To my horror, I begin to tear up. "Oh, god, sorry," I murmur, reaching for a napkin.

"What's wrong?" Allison gasps. The waiter walks over and is about to ask for our drink orders but they wave him away.

"It's…it's…" I grab a napkin to hide my face and try to take deep breaths.

"Is it a boy?" Miriam guesses.

I nod. "Nate."

"Wait, wait…not your stepbrother?" she asks incredulously. Allison glances at me and I nod at her. She turns to Miriam.

"They started, you know, seeing each other over the summer…but I guess something happened," she fills Miriam in.

"Long story short," I say, catching my breath. "Pierce is a jerk, our parents got divorced, and we broke up."

"Wow," Miriam breathes, her eyes wide. "You had quite the summer."

"Tell me about it," I say with a wry smile. "I could really use a drink." Allison flags down the waiter, and by the time our first round has arrived, my tears have stopped.

"So, can I tell you guys my own secret?" Miriam asks, leaning over the table conspiratorially. Allison and I nod. "I had sex!"

"Oh, god, now I'm the only virgin," Allison moans. "How was it?"

"Honestly…not that great the first time. But the third time, I think I had an orgasm," Miriam whispers.

"You *think*?" Allison asks, cocking her head in confusion.

"Yeah, I think. What about you, Brynn?"

"What?"

"Did you and Nate…" she trails off suggestively.

"Um, yes."

"And?" Allison leans forward.

My heartbeat quickens at the memory of his touch before sadness washes over me. I shake my head. "I'd rather not think about it."

I finish the rest of the dinner trying to engage in the conversation, but knowing that I'm often forcing the smile on my face. Allison and Miriam do their best to raise my spirits, and I try to act excited about classes starting on Monday, but my mind, and my heart, aren't quite in it.

After I pay the bill, Allison and Miriam volunteer to walk me back to my room, but I demur, feeling like a walk by myself before bed. After I hug them goodbye, I stroll along the edge of campus, watching all the action unfold as everyone enjoys the last weekend free of homework.

It's not long before I realize my feet are leading me past the crew house. *Just a quick look*, I tell myself. I begin to walk more slowly as I see it up the street. The lights are on inside the house, and I can see some people hanging out on the front porch. The late summer night has just darkened, and I stand under a street light peering up at the house. I can see several of the crew guys up there, and a petite blonde leaning on the railing with her back toward me.

The front door swings open and I press my lips together as I see Nate walk out with two bottles of beer in his hand. He's so close…just across the street and up the hill, and yet I can't be with him, this person with whom I've shared such intimate moments.

My heart stops as he smiles at the blonde. It can't be…he can't have moved on already. But there he is, offering her one of the beers, and sitting down next to her on the railing and wrapping an arm around her shoulders. A chill comes over me despite the warm air. I really am a fool.

I jump as a bottle crashes on a campus path just behind me. I glance up to see the denizens of the porch also looking at the source of the sound, and freeze for a moment as Nate stares right at me. Fuck.

I turn around, cursing myself for walking this way. I walk quickly down the street, turning right onto a path to take me into campus.

"Brynn?" I hear him call out behind me, and the sound of footsteps coming down the steps. I pick up my pace, hoping to lose him in the darkness. I can't let our first meeting after breaking up be him finding me spying on his house.

"Brynn!" I hear a woman's voice yell behind me, and almost trip over my own feet in surprise. "Brynn!" she calls again, and I turn around.

"Eileen," I say in surprise as she emerges out of the darkness, slightly out of breath. "Was...was that you up there? With Nate?" She nods, a wide smile covering her face. My eyes dart over his shoulder as I see Nate stop by the entrance to the path.

"I'm down here visiting him for the weekend," she says happily.

"Oh, oh," I murmur, covering my face in embarrassment. "I'm sorry I ran…I thought…I mean, from the back, I thought you and he were…"

"Oh!" she exclaims. "Well, I suppose I'm flattered…I mean, I do put my time in at the gym." She steps forward and takes my hands. "I'm so glad to see you Brynn. If you hadn't gotten involved, I wouldn't be here with Nate today." I try to blink back tears, but they roll down my cheeks anyway. "I'm so sorry for everything you've been through—Nate told me—"

"Mom?" Nate says, stepping forward. "Mind if I talk to Brynn alone for a minute?"

"Of course!" she calls over her shoulder, then turns to me. "It's so nice to hear him call me 'Mom,'" she says, then leans forward and whispers in my ear, "Don't give up hope." I blink at her in surprise as she pulls away and walks back toward Nate. They share a smile and a few murmured words before she continues back toward the crew house and Nate approaches me.

"Hi," he murmurs as he walks up to me.

"Hello," I reply, a bit more stiffly.

"I found her number where you left it," he explains. "We met several times while I was still up in Maryland, but it hardly seemed like enough time, so she drove me back down here and is staying for a few days." He takes a deep breath. "When you told me you loved me—"

I raise my hand to stop him. "You don't have to explain. You told me from the beginning that you didn't do relationships…that you didn't lead girls on. So I should have known. I shouldn't have expected—"

"Brynn, please. Just give me two minutes, OK?"

I nod, shifting from foot to foot as I wish I could just run away, all the way back to my room and pull the covers over my head. Anything so that I don't have to hear all the reasons why he doesn't love me.

"When you told me you loved me," he resumes, "I felt empty." Tears spring to my eyes—oof, that was worse than I thought. "No, not like that!" he says, seeing my reaction. "I mean, I felt…inadequate. Like I had nothing inside me to give back to you. Here you were, so strong, and smart, and intelligent, and I felt like such a failure." I'm shocked to hear his voice break. He clears his throat before he continues. "I had failed *you*. I felt… I mean, everything my dad had ever told me was a lie!" he exclaims, his voice rising. "In that moment, I don't think I knew if I was capable of love. What my father had shown me for years wasn't love, I don't think, it was control. I felt so undeserving to be loved by you, and for me to even tell you that I loved you, it wouldn't mean anything, because it would be from someone who was empty."

"You're not empty," I murmur, unable to hear him talk about himself like this even though he broke my heart.

"I'm starting to realize that. It's been good, seeing my mom, talking to her, hearing the truth about my past. All the things that you were trying to help me with. You were right all along."

"I wasn't trying to be right."

"I know, that's not—sorry, this is coming out all wrong. I've been thinking about you every day, imagining us meeting up back on campus, and it's just happened a lot quicker than I thought it would. I wanted to call you every day, but I needed to make sure I was ready. That I had done some work on myself before I tried to reach out to you. I know the kind of relationship I want to have with you, and I want to make sure I'm ready for it."

I blink at him, feeling confused. "So, what are you saying?"

"I'm saying that you're not my stepsister anymore, first of all," he says with a small grin. "They filed today."

"You talked to your dad?"

"Just once. I couch-surfed with friends after you left. I didn't want to stay in the same house with him."

I stare at him as a realization begins to trickle through my brain. "It was you, wasn't it? You got him to give my mom a settlement."

He runs a hand through his hair. "Well, after talking with my mom, and hearing what happened to her in their divorce, I was worried he wouldn't be fair in dealing with your mom either. So, I, um, told him that if he ever wanted to see me again, he'd have to give your mom some money in the divorce. And your tuition, well, I figured after what he put you through, that you deserved it."

"I can't believe you did that."

"Actually, I wasn't sure it would work. I mean, I wasn't sure if he wanted to see me again anyway."

"I think, in his own twisted way, he does love you."

"His *very* twisted way." He steps forward and reaches for my hand, which is still entwined in my hair. He pulls it down and laces his fingers through mine. "I can't promise you that I'll know how to be in a normal relationship right away, but please, give me another chance. I know how badly I fucked up, but I want to do better. Please. I want to learn with you."

I pause, uncertain. Can I really put myself out there with him? Risk my heart being broken again? I feel him begin to pull my hand gently behind his back so that I'm forced to take a step in. He leans forward, tucking my arm against the small of his back.

"No fair," I whisper, as the heat of his body envelopes me. He wraps his other arm around me.

"I know," he says with a sly grin. "But can you blame me? I'd do anything for another chance with you."

Everything about him is so intoxicating. I'm dizzy with desire for him after not being near him for close to a month. I turn my face up to his.

"OK, OK," I relent. "One more chance."

The words have barely left my lips when he covers my mouth with his. My legs almost give out as we touch—a mix of pleasure and relief overwhelming my body.

"God, I've missed you," he murmurs, breaking away for a moment. I pull his head back down to mine and sink my tongue into his mouth.

"Get a room!"

We break away as a group of guys, probably freshmen, walk past us, hooting and hollering. Nate glares at them for a moment, then rolls his eyes.

"Come on, there's something I've wanted to do for a long time anyway." He leads me by the hand back out of campus and across the street to the crew house. I'm wondering if he means something sexual, and worries he forgot his mom is visiting him. We walk up the steps and I see her and the crew guys turn to us as we step onto the porch. "Everyone, this is my girlfriend, Brynn," he announces proudly.

CHAPTER THIRTY

* * *

Eileen's face breaks into a huge grin as I blush. His teammates slap him on the back and needle him about his lack of previous relationships, then begin to introduce themselves to me. I'm quickly offered a beer and pulled into multiple conversations, but Nate is there every few minutes with a hand on my back, making sure I'm OK.

As the night goes on, the porch fills up with more people, and, particularly, more women. I'm happily overwhelmed by all these new faces, but also glad to just lean on the railing for a minute to sip my beer.

"Brynn?" I hear a woman's voice call. I turn to see Cara walking up onto the porch.

"Hey!" I say, and stand up to give her a hug.

"How was your summer?"

"Um…" I murmur, unable to find the words to describe the last few months. I look over her shoulder and watch a girl I don't know place her hand on Nate's chest. Before I can even frown, though, he steps back and smiles politely, then makes his way over to me. "It was pretty crazy," is all I can come up with before Nate's arm snakes his way around my waist.

"I just saw my mom yawning, so I think shc's about to go back to her hotel," he says. "Oh, hey Cara."

"Nate…are you two…?" Cara asks, her eyes darting back and forth between us.

"We are," I confirm, as Nate grins down at me. It does feel good to say it out loud.

"And you've already met his parents? Wow!"

"Yeah, we've met," I reply a bit evasively, as Nate bites his lip to keep from laughing. I elbow him in the ribs. "We better go say goodbye to his mom."

Sure enough, Eileen is shouldering her purse and looking around as we walk over.

"I hope I didn't take up too much of your time with Nate tonight," I say as we walk up.

"Not at all. I wouldn't be here at all if it weren't for you," she says, wrapping me up in a big hug. "Will you join us for brunch tomorrow before I head back home?" I glance at Nate, who's looking at me encouragingly.

"I'd love to."

"Great, I'll see you tomorrow then!" she says, giving Nate a hug before walking down the steps.

"Is it weird that I want to be friends with your mom?" I ask him as we watch her get into her car.

"Not weirder than sleeping with your stepbrother," he murmurs wickedly in my ear. "You think you've had enough of this party?"

I shiver at the implication of his words. "I think so." He nods over his shoulder toward the front door of the house and I follow him inside. The living room has several people in it now, but he continues up the steps and to his bedroom down the hall. "There isn't going to be another girl under your covers, is there?" I ask him teasingly as he opens the door.

He turns to me with a grin. "Only you now, Brynn." He wraps his arms around my waist and pulls me across the threshold, shutting the door behind me and then pressing me up against it. My body lights up with desire as his mouth covers mine and he pulls my arms over my head, keeping them pinned to the door with one hand over my wrists. I feel his other hand pulling up the hem of my summer dress as his legs push between mine. "Alright if this one's a little quick?" he asks, nibbling on my ear.

"I just want to feel you," I breathe, arching my back and pressing my breasts onto his chest. With a grunt, he pulls away, reaching into his pocket. I pull my dress over my head as he yanks his zipper down and pushes his boxers and khakis to his knees, rolling the condom over his length. I barely manage to get my panties to the floor when he steps back into me, grabbing my ass and hoisting me up.

I moan as I feel his tip press against my opening. I must have tightened up a bit in the time we've spent apart because there's a shot of pain as he slides me down his shaft. I wrap my arms around the back of his neck and lock my ankles just above his ass as he leans me back against the door.

"Oh fuck," he murmurs as he reaches his depth inside me. He circles his hips, letting me feel him inside me at every angle before pulling back out again. I marvel at his strength as he's able to hold me in place and thrust in and out of me with almost no support from me. The pain is gone by just his third thrust, and pleasure begins to course through my veins. My toes curl and I run my hands through his hair, then lean forward and slide my tongue inside his mouth.

To my surprise, he steps away from the door, wrapping one arm around my back to keep me supported. He sinks down onto the edge of his bed so that I'm sitting on top of him. I unlock my ankles and move my legs so that I'm kneeling on the mattress. I rise up onto my knees as he leans back on his hands, getting used to the feeling of riding him. I reach my arms back, bringing my hands to the top of his thighs as I slide down him, feeling him stretching me open.

He's hitting me in all the right places and I begin to move faster and faster. I keep my eyes open, watching as his mouth drops open and his jaw clenches. I love seeing that I'm pushing him right to the edge even as an orgasm is quickly building inside of me. His hips begin to pick up off the bed, slamming into me as I sink down. The extra power is just what I need, and I feel myself explode on top of him just as he begins to cry out. I keep rising up and down as I come, feeling how slick I am inside. He pulls me tight against him, resting his head between my breasts, as we both take deep, gasping breaths.

But he's not done yet. I feel his hands creep up to my bra strap, unhooking it and sliding it down my arms. Even though I'm exhausted, I lean back and lift up my arms so he can slide it all the way off. He tosses it onto a nearby chair then sighs and runs his fingers down my neck, across my clavicle, then down my shoulders.

"I missed you," he murmurs kissing me softly in the middle of my chest. I bend my head down and kiss his hairline, then reach down and tug at his shirt. He obediently lifts his arms up so I can slide it off.

"Mm," I mutter as I lean forward against him, relishing the skin-to-skin contact. Suddenly I feel him lift me up and turn me around, depositing me with my back on the bed. He reaches down to hold the condom on as he pulls out of me, grabbing a tissue from his side table and finally kicking his pants and underwear all the way off.

He slides back next to me on the bed as I glance around his room. It's neat in here, as I'd expect, except for floor-to-ceiling shelves next to his metal desk that are overflowing with textbooks.

"Had to have them put in," he says, seeing me looking at them. "But I'll give you the tour later." I feel his hand slide over my hips, pulling me toward him. That hand slowly inches down as his tongue slides against mine, now working slowly, his urgency gone. He groans as he feels the wetness between my legs and slides one finger inside me. His thumb just grazes my clit and I gasp, pressing back against him. "Do I still get to order you around in bed?"

"Yes, please," I whimper, closing my eyes as he begins to circle his thumb.

"Good," he murmurs, and his fingers pull away, but are immediately replaced by his mouth. I moan as he takes a long lick of me, pulling my legs apart and repositioning his body between them. He holds my knees out wide, opening me to him completely. His tongue moves down to my opening, darting in and out of me—such a different sensation than his fingers or his cock. As he moves up again to my clit, flicking his tongue mercilessly back and forth across it, I feel another orgasm begin to pool deep in my belly.

"Wait, wait, come here," I say, touching his hand on my knee. "I want to taste you, too." He looks up at me with a grin, and sits up. I press my legs together and he works his way up my body on his knees. I pin my arms to my sides as he comes up and kneels on either side of my shoulders. I pick up my head and he takes his hard cock in his hand, placing it between my lips. I can taste the latex of the condom we just used, mixed with both of our own scents.

"Fuck, Brynn," he growls as he slowly presses his hips forward until his cock hits the back of my throat. He begins to move a little faster, but he's careful not to overwhelm me, knowing that I'm completely helpless under him. I keep my eyes on his face as sweat begins to break out on his brow and his neck muscles tense. With a groan, he pulls out of my mouth. "Turn over," he orders me as he swings one leg over me so that I can follow his command.

I obey, feeling my breasts squish against the plain blue comforter. I hear the rip of another condom and a moment later he lies down on top of me, sweeping my hair off the back of my neck as he does so. I feel his breath on my ear as his cock pushes inside me. I'm so wet and he drives deep inside— maybe it's the position, but I don't know if I've ever felt him so deep before. He pulls out and moves back in slowly, eliciting a long cry from me. I feel tears spring to my eyes at the intensity of the sensation.

"Squeeze your legs together," he whispers. I inch them together, feeling my muscles clench even more tightly around his dick. His legs are on either side of me now, and I can feel that he has more traction as he thrusts in harder now. His tongue finds my ear and my body begins to shake as his tongue flicks inside me. I hear myself begin to moan as though it's coming from someone else, though I also feel completely at one with my body and his. "Yes, yes, fuck," he grunts on top of me. "Come with me, come with me!"

I have no choice but to obey again, unraveling beneath him as he releases himself inside me. After a few final strokes, I feel him let go of his weight, relaxing on top of me. His nose nuzzles into the side of my cheek, his lips just finding the edge of my mouth to give me a kiss.

"You know what the best part is?" he whispers.

"Mm?" I murmur back, my tired brain unable to follow his train of thought.

"You can stay the night."

EPILOGUE

* * *

"Man, I'm glad this place has central air," I say, setting down the last of the boxes in our new apartment. I'm sweating even with it on, and use the bottom of my t-shirt to wipe my forehead.

"Yeah, I thought Boston was supposed to be cooler than Virginia," Nate says, shaking his head with a smile as he hoists a box onto the counter as though it weighed nothing, though I know for a fact it has our heavy dishes in it.

We flew up here for a weekend last month to find an apartment, and were quite lucky that this Charlestown two-bedroom was just our third stop. The realtor described the neighborhood as "up-and-coming," and Nate loved the cozy feel and exposed brick. Neither of us start our jobs in town for another week, but I'm glad we came early. We have all the unpacking to do, we still need a lot of furniture…

"Are you going to get tired of me?" Nate asks, walking over and wrapping his arms around my waist.

"Living together, you mean? Absolutely. Are you going to get sick of me?"

"Absolutely," he says, nodding seriously, then he grins. "I love you."

"I love you, too," I reply as he leans in to kiss me. Once such a big deal for him to say, Nate now tells me he loves me regularly. I squirm happily as his tongue darts quickly against mine. A year later, and his kisses still make me weak in the knees. "What's that box?" I ask as he releases me and I glance over his shoulder.

"Which?" he asks, looking around.

"There," I say, pointing to a medium-sized box sitting where we plan to put the couch, when we get one.

"Dunno," he says with a shrug. "Clothes?"

"Mm, no, I don't think so," I reply, walking over to it and picking it up. "It's really light." I shake it and can just hear the crinkling of paper. "That's weird." I set it back down on the floor and kneel next to it, scratching at the corner of the packing tape sealing it shut. I finally get enough up to get my finger under it, and pull it across the boxes flaps. Nick comes to stand near me as I pull it open. "I really don't remember packing this one, but maybe I'm going crazy."

It has been an eventful week. We graduated last weekend, and played host to both of our moms, and then just a few days later we were driving up to Boston. We both managed to secure jobs here, Nate with a historical society, and me in the research side of a non-profit. I pull the brown packing paper out of the box, piling it on the floor next to me.

"Oh dear, did I pack an empty box?" I ask, just as my fingers close around a much smaller box at the bottom of the larger one. "What's…" my eyes widen as I realize I'm holding a jewelry box. I glance up at Nate, who's grinning at me. He kneels down onto the hardwood floor next to me. "Oh my god," I murmur, as he takes the small box out of my hands. Of course we've discussed marriage, but I didn't think he would propose so soon.

"Brynn," he whispers, "I've come alive since I met you. My world before you came into it was cold and dark, and then you showed up and brought light into it. Every day, I find a new reason to fall more in love with you. I know we're still young, but I want so much to have the honor of calling you my wife. Will you marry me?" he asks, opening the box. I stare at the simple, beautiful diamond ring sitting in the middle of the red velvet box as my eyes fill with tears.

"Yes, yes, of course I'll marry you," I gasp, wrapping my arms around his neck and covering him with kisses. He laughs joyously and lifts me off the ground with his free arm.

"Here, try it on," he finally says. "I measured your ring finger while you were sleeping."

"Sneaky!" I tease him as he slips the ring on my hand. "It's a perfect fit," I say, holding it toward the nearest window so the light catches it.

"Should we call your mom?" he asks, wrapping his arms back around my waist.

"Let's wait until tomorrow. For today, only you and I will know."

"Only you," he echoes, pressing his forehead against mine. "Only you."

THE END

* * *

Connect with Colleen Masters and other Hearts Collective authors online at: http://www.Hearts-Collective.com, Facebook, Twitter. To keep in touch and for information on new releases!

If you enjoyed *Stepbrother Untouchable*, be sure to check out *Stepbrother Billionaire* by Colleen Masters. Now Available on Amazon!

* * *

I've hated him since middle school.

The effortlessly popular, lacrosse superstar, beautiful, blue-eyed nightmare Emerson Sawyer. Funny thing is, he didn't even know I existed until our senior year, when his mom started hooking up with my dad.

Now he torments me in the hallways, calling me "Sis" whenever he gets the chance, relishing in the fact that I can't hide my blushing whenever he's around. Even though I can't stand him, my body betrays me—and he loves it.

Emerson and his mom just moved in with us, and as if crushing on him wasn't weird enough, now our bedrooms share a wall.

The sexual tension keeps building between us, but I know nothing can ever happen…especially now that our parents are engaged. I try to tell myself that I hate him, that he's wrong for me, that we'll never be together…

So why did I agree to play Seven Minutes in Heaven at his girlfriend's high school party?

And why does Emerson suddenly have my panties in his hands?

Stepbrother Billionaire is a Stand-alone novel. It contains adult themes, harsh language, and graphic sexual content.

GET IT NOW AMAZON

14644651R00198

Printed in Great Britain
by Amazon.co.uk, Ltd.,
Marston Gate.